# IN THE WAKE OF
# HANNIBAL

# IN THE WAKE OF
# HANNIBAL

ROBIN LEVIN

ISBN: 978-0-692-67744-5

This book is a work of fiction. Any resemblance to actual persons, living or dead, events or locales is entirely coincidental.

Printed by Ingram Spark

Typesetting and cover design by www.wordzworth.com

# CONTENTS

# INTRODUCTION

In my previous book, the Death of Carthage, I related the story of the Second Punic War, between Rome and Carthage, from the point of view of the Romans. In this book I tell the story from the point of view of the Carthaginians. This book, In the Wake of Hannibal, covers the Second Punic War, the sixteen year long struggle in which the Carthaginian general Hannibal invades Italy, wins battle after battle but is defeated in the end.

The story is related by Hannibal's younger brother Mago, by Mago's childhood friend, Gisco, and by Gisco's Spanish wife, Sansara. Mago is utterly devoted to his brother Hannibal, and Gisco is utterly devoted to Mago-until the day comes when he is ordered by the priest of the Goddess Tanit and the God Baal Hammon to sacrifice his five month old son Hanno as a burnt offering to the Gods. Faced with an impossible dilemma, Gisco chooses to save his son by defecting to the Romans.

The question arises as to whether or not the ancient Carthaginians practiced human sacrifice. This is still a matter of controversy, but I think that the preponderance of the evidence indicates that they did. There have been found cemeteries, sometimes called "tophets," in or near Carthage that contain urns bearing the remains of children aged from birth to three years old. DNA analysis of these remains indicate that the children were all male. Accounts of Carthage written by ancient Greeks also describe the practice of sacrificing children. How common the practice was is difficult to say, but some scholars believe that it was more common in times of stress, and that the practice continued up until the time of the destruction of Carthage in 146 B.C. In this book I present Hannibal and his brothers as being strongly opposed to the practice of infant sacrifice. It is reasonable that Hannibal would oppose the practice if for no other reason than that he believed that Carthage should be strong militarily, and sacrificing male infants deprived the state of future soldiers.

My most influential source of inspiration in writing this novel was Titus Livius, commonly called Livy, who wrote *Ab Urbe Condita*, a history of Rome. I would not have started this project if I had not been exposed to the works of Livy, and I think my readers will benefit by making an acquaintance with this ancient writer. There were a number of modern sources that were helpful in providing useful information for this work, particularly B. H. Liddle Hart's *Scipio Africanus: Greater than Napoleon*, and Jacob Abbott's *Hannibal–The Greatest Commander*. Other sources are listed in the Bibliography. I give thanks to my brother Robert D. Levin for his encouragement, and my nieces Janna Levin and Suzanne Levin for their encouragement and support. Finally, I wish to thank Sunah Cherwin, my editor, for her assistance in editing this work.

# TIMELINE FOR
# IN THE WAKE OF HANNIBAL

264 B.C.    Beginning of the First Punic War.

247 B.C.    Birth of Hannibal Barca.

245 B.C.    Birth of Hasdrubal Barca (Approximate.)

243 B.C.    Birth of Mago Barca (Approximate.)

241 B.C.    End of First Punic War. Peace treaty on Roman terms.

228 B.C.    Hamilcar Barca, Father of Hannibal, Hasdrubal and Mago, dies in battle in Spain. His son-in-law Hasdrubal the Fair comes to power. Hasdrubal the Fair founds Khart Hadasht (New Carthage.)

220 B.C.    Hasdrubal the Fair is assassinated by a Gaul. Hannibal Barca comes to power. Gisco's daughter Giscana is born.

219 B.C.    Hannibal lays siege to Saguntum.

218 B.C.    Rome declares war on Carthage, beginning the Second Punic War. Hannibal takes his army over the Alps. Battles of the Ticinus and the Trebia, both decisive Carthaginian victories.

217 B.C.    Battle of Trasimene. Decisive Carthaginian victory. Gisco's son Gisco is born.

216 B.C.    Battle of Cannae. Decisive Carthaginian victory. Over 50,000 Roman and allied soldiers killed.

215 B.C.    Mago returns to Carthage to try to persuade the Carthaginian Senate to send supplies and reinforcements to Hannibal. Battle of Dertosa, decisive Roman victory. Mago is sent with an army back to Spain rather than to Italy.

214 B.C.    Gisco's son Hanno is born, Gisco defects to the Romans.

211 B.C.    Battles of the Upper Baetis. Decisive Carthaginian victories. Both Publius Cornelius Scipio and his Brother Cneius Cornelius Scipio are killed. Gisco and his family are abducted from Tarraco and Gisco rejoins Mago.

210 B.C.    Publius Cornelius Scipio, the son of the Publius Cornelius Scipio who died at the Battle of the Upper Baetis becomes proconsul in Spain.

209 B.C.    Publius Cornelius Scipio conquers Khart Hadasht (New Carthage.)

207 B.C.    Hasdrubal Barca, brother of Hannibal leads his army over the Alps and invades Italy. He and his army are destroyed by the Romans at the Battle of the Metaurus.

206 B.C.    Battle of Ilipa. Decisive Roman victory. All of Spain now in the hands of the Romans

205 B.C.    Mago Barca brings an army by ship to Liguria, but is unable to get through Roman lines to join Hannibal.

202 B.C.    Publius Cornelius Scipio invades Africa. Hannibal and Mago are both recalled to Carthage by the Carthaginian Senate. Mago is wounded in battle shortly before he sails from Italy and dies during the passage. Battle of Zama: Decisive Roman victory. Peace treaty on Roman terms.

# Prologue



Gisco
Tarraco, Spain, 211 B.C.

I wonder how long it will take me to die, once nailed to the cross. Mago said that it sometimes takes days. I wonder if they are taking me to Khart Hadasht to be crucified on the *Byrsa* on the same spot the assassin of Hasdrubal the Fair had been. Will I be able to show the same fortitude as the Celt? He may have been made of sterner stuff then I. He was crucified for murder, and I will be crucified for the crime I committed in trying to save my child.

I'm no stranger to violence. I'm a soldier and I've killed many men in battle. It was my duty but I tried to be decent about it. I always tried to kill the enemy as quickly as possible and not make him suffer. I will receive no such mercy. It occurs to me that my brother will watch my execution. He'll be furious at me for the disgrace I have brought upon him and our family. I hope I will not disgrace him further by acting as a coward in the face of death.

How could it have come to a choice between my country and my child? What god could be so cruel? Men will say I made the wrong choice, but there was no other choice I could make. At least this way I will go to my death with my self-respect intact.

# ONE

## The Death of the Assassin

Gisco
Khart Hadasht (New Carthage), Spain, 221 B.C.

Gisco!"

I recognized the voice calling me. It belonged to Mago, my friend since early childhood. I turned to greet him. His expression was serious, a contrast to his usual levity. He was dressed in the fashion of a Carthaginian nobleman with a white robe flowing down to his ankles, heavily embroidered with gold and purple thread depicting sacred animals and plants. His feet were shod in beaded leather sandals. I was clad in a simple soldier's tunic.

"My brother wants everyone to witness the execution of the assassin. It begins at midday," he said.

I had never witnessed a crucifixion up close before. I was not sure that I wanted to do so now, but duty called. "Do we have to stay for the whole thing?" I asked.

"No," said Mago, "It will take him hours, maybe even days, to die. Hannibal has forbidden anything that might shorten the process, such as breaking his legs. It must be a fitting punishment for the man who slew our brother-in-law, Hasdrubal the Fair."

Mago's brother, Hannibal, only twenty-six years old, was now the most powerful man in Carthaginian Spain. He had been elected *Rab Mahanet,* or supreme general, by the Carthaginian assembly. His first duty as successor to his brother-in-law was to conduct Hasdrubal the Fair's funeral rites. His second task was to see to the execution of the assassin.

"The crucifixion will take place on the Byrsa." said Mago. "It will be visible to the whole city, but you and I will get a close view. Your brother Drubal is already there, along with my brother Hasdrubal and our cousin Maharbal." My brother's name was actually Hasdrubal but Mago and I called him Drubal to distinguish him from Mago's brother Hasdrubal. Drubal hated the abbreviation but we did it anyway, partly to annoy him, I suppose.

I followed Mago to the citadel that we called the Byrsa. We had to climb up many flights of steps. There were temples to Melqart and Tanit and *Ba-al Hammon,* to Eshmoun and to Ishtar, as well as a magnificent shrine to honor the memory of Elissa, the founder of Carthage. All the temples were newly completed. Hasdrubal the Fair had founded New Carthage only eight years before his death. It was a beautiful city with a splendid harbor. I much preferred it to old Carthage, and if I had had my way I would have lived my whole life there. The city was surrounded by high walls and was thought to be impregnable. The late spring day was pleasantly warm, without a cloud in the sky. The assassin had picked a magnificent day to die.

The assassin was a Celt with sandy hair, a reddish beard and the most striking blue eyes. He was well above average height and solidly built. He was lying on his back, naked except for a loincloth, his hands and feet bound to the wooden cross. He had been scourged and his back was weeping fluid. His facial expression was one of contempt rather than fear. I could see that, whatever the reason for his deed, he did not regret it.

Mago's brother Hannibal stood up to speak about the deceased. "Our brother-in-law, Hasdrubal the Fair, was a noble son of Carthage. He was also a true friend to all the peoples of Spain. Eight years ago he founded this magnificent city of Khart Hadasht, and then he proceeded to bring the blessings of civilization to this primitive land. He joyfully extended Carthage's hand in friendship to anyone willing to receive it. We sorely missed our father, Hamilcar Barca, who was killed in war with the Carpetani, but Hasdrubal the Fair followed admirably in his footsteps. I, Hannibal Barca, pledge to continue Hasdrubal's work and expand upon it. We will make all of Spain part of Carthage's realm. If the Romans oppose us, we will deal with them with an iron hand. We now take this opportunity to demonstrate, for all to see, the fate of any who stand in our way. This depraved murderer will now pay the penalty for his deeds."

Hannibal signaled to his executioner, Memon, who brought forth his hammer and spikes. Memon knelt by the cross and hammered the first spike through the assassin's right wrist and deep into the wood. The Celt grimaced and grunted but did not scream. Memon proceeded to the left side and hammered the second spike into the wrist. Then he hammered spikes through of the assassin's two feet, fastening them to the wood. Blood seeped from the wounds but did not gush. Memon knew how to avoid the larger vessels. The man's agony was evident on his face, but still he did not cry out. Memon then gestured to his assistants who lifted up the wooden cross, with the assassin firmly attached, and planted it in the hole they had dug for it. The body was now suspended several feet above the ground. I stared at his face. His blue eyes met mine and I felt a wave of pain and nausea, as though he were able to transmit his suffering to me. My brother Drubal was standing nearby. He grinned.

"You look ill, Gisco," he said.

I didn't want him to think I was squeamish so I said, "Something I ate last night, maybe those eels from the lagoon." He laughed. We both knew I was lying.

Mago took me by the arm. "Let's go have some bread and wine." I followed him down to Hasdrubal the Fair's palace where we both had our quarters. Hasdrubal had no sons, so now the palace belonged to Hannibal. We went to Mago's quarters and stretched out on couches. Mago signaled a slave to bring us bread, fruit and wine. "How is your wife?" he asked me.

"She seems to be over the morning sickness now," I said. "I think the baby will be born in another four or five months."

"You don't seem all that enthusiastic about it," he said.

"Oh, Sansara's a sweet girl," I said, "but she struggles to learn Phoenician and I fear we may never be able to communicate. Hasdrubal the Fair arranged this marriage with the daughter of the chieftain of the Volciani for his own political ends. I had no choice in the matter. Sometimes I wish I could have married a Carthaginian girl whom I could at least speak to. We can make love, but, to me it's not really a marriage if you can't communicate with your woman. I want someone who can cheer me when I'm feeling bad, and can share my happiness with me when I triumph. I want the sort of marriage my father and mother have.

"I know what you mean," agreed Mago. "There's more to marriage than lust. Now that Hasdrubal is dead I plan to put aside my wife. I'll make a visit to Carthage and find a nice girl there."

"Hannibal might have something to say about that," I said. "Would he want to offend your wife's father, the chief of the Turditani?"

Mago looked irritated. "Hannibal doesn't run my life!" he proclaimed.

"That's where you're wrong, Mago," I laughed. "Hannibal runs everyone's life."

Mago sighed in acknowledgement of the truth of my statement. "We won't be enjoying this good life here in Khart Hadasht much longer if Hannibal has his way. He has plans." He broke off a large piece of bread and dipped it in olive oil. He poured a glass of wine for each of us. The crucifixion had taken away my appetite and I limited myself to sipping wine.

"What are his plans?" I asked.

Mago looked around him to be sure no one else was listening. "You will tell no one," he said.

I nodded.

"You are the only one I would trust with this information, Gisco." He spoke softly. "I love both of my brothers, but you are like my twin. We have been friends as long as I can remember." He paused. "Hannibal plans to lay siege to Saguntum. He's gathering up forces from the Spanish tribes and training them. He's also employing Greek engineers from Massilia to design siege engines that can break down their walls."

The wine I had been sipping went down badly and I started to cough. When I finally got control of myself I said, "Saguntum? But that's an ally of Rome!"

"That's the whole point!" said Mago. "Hannibal wants to start another war with Rome!"

I stared at Mago in disbelief. "Hannibal thinks he can defeat Rome?"

"If anyone can defeat Rome, it would be Hannibal," said Mago. "My brother is brilliant. The Romans are brave, stubborn, and persistent. They fight to the death. But they have no great imagination, no cunning. Hannibal will easily outmaneuver them in battle. It will be a fascinating spectacle to behold! I will be going with him when we invade Italia. You should come too. When we conquer Rome we'll be masters of the world!"

I thought of Sansara and the coming child. Despite my complaints about her inability to speak Phoenician, I loved her dearly.

She was a willing and able bed partner. This would mean that I would have to leave her and risk losing her. On the other hand, I could not imagine leaving Mago's side. We had been friends ever since I could remember. Besides, I was a man and a soldier of Carthage, and I knew that I had a duty to my country. We spent the rest of the afternoon chatting about hunting, fishing, warfare, games and women, all normal and appropriate pursuits for young men. We had our whole lives ahead of us. I should have been joyful, but I had a nagging suspicion that I was about to be lured into an ordeal from which I might never recover.

## SANSARA
## KHART HADASHT, 221 B.C.

I felt the baby kick today for the first time. I am excited but also afraid. Many women do not survive childbirth; so much can go wrong, and I've heard that it is exceedingly painful. But I really do want this baby; it will be so wonderful see his little face, his tiny hands. Or maybe it will be a girl. No matter. I will love her madly. It is hot tonight and I am so anxious I can't sleep. Gisco is still away, out drinking and playing draughts with Mago. Gisco is kind to me, he gives me clothes and jewels and anything I ask for, but it is difficult to be married when we don't speak the same language. I am lonely here in Kart Hadasht and only my friendship with Imilce keeps me sane.

Only a year ago I was just an ordinary girl in my village. My mother called me to her one day and said that Grandfather wanted to talk to me. She took me to his lodge and I knelt before him. His lodge was like the others in the village, a round wooden structure with a hearth in the center and an opening at the top for smoke to emerge, but his was larger than most. The walls were lined with swords, shields, spears, helmets and war horns. Wolf pelts and stag's antlers were also on display. Grandfather drank wine from a cup made from a human skull, lined with gold leaf. He had been a fierce warrior in his younger days and now he was chieftain of our tribe, the Volciani. He was over sixty years old, still tall, lean and fit. He wore a mustache that drooped down at the sides of his mouth.

He motioned for me to sit on a stool. "Sansara, my child, I'm sure that you know that as my granddaughter you must do whatever I say and obey my counsel in all things."

"Yes, Grandfather," I replied.

"What I'm about to tell you may not be to your liking, but you are fifteen now and a very smart girl. I feel that I should explain to you how things are and why we must do things that we may not want to do."

This did not sound promising. I could feel my heart begin to race. I looked up at him and saw love and concern on his face. I returned my gaze to the floor. "Yes Grandfather."

"Do you remember your father, Sansara?" he asked. "Do you recall how he died?"

"Yes, Grandfather," I said, "he was killed in a battle against the Carthaginians."

"Yes," said Grandfather. "We Volciani were in an alliance with the Carpetani, and we went to war when the Carthaginian leader, Hamilcar, tried to extend his rule over our tribes. Your father was killed in that war. But Hamilcar was killed in one of the battles against the Carpetani and his place has been taken by a man they call Hasdrubal the Fair. This Hasdrubal seems to have a different policy than Hamilcar. He has offered the Volciani and other tribes alliances based on friendship and mutual interest. I don't know how far to trust this Hasdrubal, but I am weary of burying sons, nephews and cousins. I am weary of trying to provide for widows. I have decided to accept Hasdrubal's offer and I have persuaded our tribal council to support this decision. It seems inevitable that the Carthaginians will eventually rule all of Spain and it seems to me that it is better to make an accommodation with them than to risk annihilation and slavery."

He paused to give me a chance to think about his words. Finally I said: "I know little of these matters, Grandfather, but I am sure you are right."

"So where do you come in, Sansara?" he asked. "Hasdrubal has made alliances with a number of Spanish tribes, the Turditani, the Illergites, the Ausetani, the Seditani, and others. He likes to cement these alliances with a marriage of a well-born maiden to one of his kinsmen. I have offered you in marriage to one of his nephews, a young man named Gisco."

I was speechless. I just stared at him open-mouthed. This marriage would mean the complete end of the life I had always known, an irrevocable change in every facet of my life, a cataclysm of the greatest magnitude.

Seeing my look of panic and my inability to respond, he leaned forward and placed his hands on my shoulders, "I can see that you aren't ready to contemplate this matter. We will talk again in a few days. Just bear in mind that there are some things in life that we can't avoid. I want you to be strong and do your duty to your family and to your tribe. This alliance will mean much for the survival of the Volciani. No more will our little girls lose their fathers, and our women lose their husbands. Sometimes you must make sacrifices for the good of your people. You may go now. I'm sure you will want to discuss this with your mother."

I walked out of the lodge and into the sunlight. Mama was waiting for me. "Mama," I cried, "Grandfather says I must leave here, that I must marry a Carthaginian, someone I don't know, whose language I don't speak!"

"Yes, I know, my beloved." She put her arms around me. "Sometimes circumstances compel us to do things we don't want to do. You won't be the first young girl to be compelled to marry outside of her own tribe. You know that my mother was Arevaci, and when she came here she did not speak our language and had to learn it. By the time she died she was one of the most respected women in our village. If you are open to new experiences this could be a great opportunity for you. You will be marrying a rich man, you will have fine clothes, food, and lodgings there, things that we, who live on the Tagus, have only heard about from traveler's tales."

"But what if I don't like him?" I asked. "Or what if he doesn't like me? What if he rejects me in favor of a girl who can speak his language?"

"Listen to me, child," she said, "I have been married twice, to your father and to your stepfather Manolo. Words do not bind a man to you. The bed is where you prove your worth to a man. If you can delight and fascinate him in bed, he will always come back to you for more. The first time with a man is painful, but once you get over that, your congress can be very pleasurable. Figure out what pleases him, how he likes to be touched and stroked. Be an eager partner in his games. I'm telling you this because this is your one chance to make the best of this situation."

I could scarcely believe my mother was saying these words to me. She was a modest and respectable matron. "I will try to remember your advice, Mama," I replied. "I hope I can bring myself to follow it."

"If you were a boy, I might soon be sending you off to do battle," said Mama. "Now I'm sending you off to do battle of a different sort. You must be brave, Sansara."

A few weeks later a delegation from Khart Hadasht came to escort me to their city. Everyone in the village came out to wish me farewell. I hugged each of my close friends and kinswomen and we all wept. Grandfather asked my stepfather, Manolo, to accompany our party and to see that I was well treated and my needs were met. We traveled by horseback; the journey took over a week. Finally we reached a walled city and were admitted through a large wooden gate.

I was awed by the grandeur of the city. There was a citadel with huge temples, and even most of the ordinary buildings were three and four levels. Mama was right, everything was beyond what a country girl could imagine—paintings, statues, sculptures, fine cloth garments—I could not help staring at everything with my mouth hanging open. I must have seemed like an idiot. I had entered a different world, one that would take all my wit and strength to adapt to. The worst thing about it was that I had been deprived of the power of speech. After Manolo left there would be no one I could talk to.

I was taken to a grand palace made of marble. We entered a vast hall decorated with paintings and statues. Some of the paintings depicted battle scenes; others appeared to show gods feasting;

still others, men on horseback hunting with their dogs. A woman servant took me by the arm and began chattering at me, clucking and shaking her head. She led me to a bath house. I had never seen a bath house before, but had always bathed in the Tagus River. She removed my clothes and bade me step into the pool. The water was steaming. I was afraid I would be scalded, but after a few minutes it became comfortable. She rubbed my body with a pleasant-smelling lotion—I thought that it had the essence of some type of flower, but it was not one that I recognized. She rubbed another sort of lotion into my hair and rinsed it out.

When the servant was satisfied that I was clean, she motioned for me to get out of the tub and rubbed my body dry with a cloth. Then she helped me don a pretty robe embroidered with flowers and intricate patterns. She combed and braided my hair. She chattered and chattered but I understood nothing.

Finally, she bade me to accompany her and led me to a chamber where three women were sitting on ornate couches doing embroidery. She introduced me but the only words I understood were "Sansara" and "Volciani." Seeing me, they all stood up, and I knelt before them. One of the women appeared to be in her early thirties. She had an olive complexion, black hair, brown eyes, and a stern demeanor. The second, a lovely woman with auburn hair and blue eyes, was about twenty-one, and the third, plump and ruddy faced with long brown braids, appeared to be about eighteen. All three of them were dressed in fine cotton robes of bright colors and elaborate embroidery, reaching down to their ankles.

To my surprise, the second one spoke to me in a language that, while somewhat different from my own, was close enough that I could understand most of what she said. She motioned for me to rise.

"Welcome, Sansara of the Volciani," she spoke slowly. "I am Imilce, sister-in-law to Hasdrubal the Fair. I come from Castulo. Do you understand my speech?"

"Yes, Madam," I said. "I am grateful that someone here can speak with me."

She indicated the older woman. "This is Saponibal, the wife of Hasdrubal, and this is Enidia, the wife of Saponibal's brother Mago. She is from the Turditani people. I am the wife of Saponibal's brother Hannibal."

"I am happy to meet you, Imilce," I said. "Please tell Saponibal and Enidia that I am happy to meet them too."

She spoke to the others and they nodded. I could see from Saponibal's expression that she thought me well beneath her.

"Tomorrow you will meet Gisco, who is to become your husband," Imilce said. "Don't worry; he is a gentleman. He will treat you well. Come and sit with us. The servants will be bringing dinner soon." She took me by the hand and led me to a couch.

The dinner was richer and more bountiful than anything I had ever eaten in my village. There was a thick porridge of peas and beans, pheasant flavored with spices I had never tasted, fish covered with a creamy sauce, warm soft leavened wheat bread, wine, and a dessert made from wheat, honey, almonds, and dates. And this was just an ordinary meal here. I wondered what a feast would be like.

After dinner Imilce showed me to my bedroom. The bed was covered with a soft down-filled mattress and there were cushions and pillows, all elaborately embroidered. There was a table and chair and on the table was an elaborate hand-held mirror. The wooden furnishings were decorated with carvings and polished to a shine. They looked as if they had been wrought by expert craftsmen. "Oh, Imilce, everything here is so beautiful, so fine!"

Imilce smiled, "This must shock you, Sansara, but you'll get used to it. Carthage is the biggest and wealthiest city in the world and the Carthaginians like finery."

"What's this?" I asked, picking up the mirror. I stared at myself. I had never seen my image in a mirror before. "So this is what people see when they look at me!" I said. I had small, regular features, straight teeth, green eyes and brown hair. I was relieved to see nothing objectionable.

"You're a pretty girl," said Imilce. "Gisco will like you. We can put some makeup on you to make your eyes stand out. They're a lovely shade of green. Saponibal, Enidia, and I will each give you something of ours to wear for now. Once you're married I'm sure Gisco will provide you with a fine wardrobe.

"Can you tell me about Gisco?" I asked.

"What can I say about Gisco?" She said. "Of all the men here, he is the one I trust most. He has an innocence about him. There is nothing devious. You can easily read his thoughts in his facial expressions and gestures. He is completely loyal to my brother-in-law Mago. They've been best friends since early childhood. But Mago is a leader and Gisco a follower. Don't expect him to be overly ambitious. You may be better off without an ambitious husband, Sansara. My Hannibal is a most ambitious man. I fear that when he comes to power, heaven and earth will tremble."

"It must be interesting being married to such a man." I said.

"Interesting, yes," she replied, "but not always comfortable. I fear that the day will come when he will be so engrossed in his endeavors that I will have no place in his life."

The next day we were invited to a feast. Imilce loaned me a fetching robe, bound up my hair, and lined my eyes with makeup in the Carthaginian style. "Let me give you some jewelry to wear," she said. "Do you know what we say in Castulo? 'A woman without jewels is like a night without stars!'" She went to her chamber and returned bearing silver bracelets and a pendant studded with rubies.

We were admitted to a large hall arrayed with couches. I had never seen so many people assembled in one place. There must have been two or three hundred people present for the feast, everyone dressed in the most ornate fashion. I felt entirely out of place, but Imilce seemed to know everyone and, taking my arm, she led me to the couch whereon sat Gisco, my husband to be. Imilce said something to Gisco and he rose. His smile showed his dimples and his gaze fastened on mine. He took my hand. I could see that he liked what he saw. I was attracted to him as well. He was not exactly what the ideal man would look like among the Volciani. Most Volciani women would have preferred someone like Manolo, who was tall, fair, and powerfully muscled, with fine sculpted features. Gisco was nearly a head shorter than Manolo, and had olive skin, curly black hair, and brown eyes. But he was not bad looking. I found him attractive and appealing. Gisco addressed me and Imilce translated. "He says he is happy to meet you; that you are very pretty, and he can't wait to get to know you better." I smiled at him and told Imilce to tell him I was happy to meet him too. He said something to Imilce and she took me to a nearby couch where Enidia was seated with a man who appeared to be about Gisco's age. "This is my brother-in-law, Mago," said Imilce, "Enidia's husband." Mago and Enidia rose and Mago bowed and kissed my hand. Imilce translated his words, "Welcome to Khart Hadasht, Sansara. I'm sure that you will make my friend Gisco very happy." I smiled and murmured that it was a pleasure to meet him. Imilce translated. My inability to speak the language made me feel awkward. I don't know what I would have done without Imilce. I had not lost my powers of observation, however, and what I observed from subtle expressions was that, while Gisco was attracted to me, Mago was not enamored of Enidia, nor she of him. I could see that their marriage was not desired or comfortable on either part.

The room suddenly became silent and everyone stood up from their couches as two distinguished-looking men made their way to a platform at the left end of the hall. The elder was a tall, handsome, bearded man, dressed in an elaborate purple robe. The younger, perhaps in his mid-twenties, was dressed in Carthaginian military regalia. The older man smiled and began to speak in a loud clear voice to the assembled crowd. Of course I understood nothing, but everyone else listened with rapt attention, appearing to hang on to his every word. I hear him say "Gisco" and Gisco grinned with pleasure. When he was finished speaking, Gisco took my hand and led me toward the podium. He said something to the crowd and everyone clapped and cheered. I understood that he was introducing me to all his friends and telling them that he planned to marry me. I could only stand there and smile politely. He led me back to our couch and Imilce explained, "The older man is Hasdrubal the Fair, and the younger one is my husband, Hannibal."

In the center of the room were tables covered with all manner of food. The end of Hasdrubal's speech signaled the start of the feast, and guests lined up to view the selection and take what delicacies they fancied. There were meats, fowl, fishes and other seafood, vegetables, breads, cheeses, wines, fruits, and desserts. I had never seen such a variety of food. Gisco took my hand and led me to one of the tables. He gave me a plate and pointed to this dish and that, apparently making recommendations. I smiled at him and took his advice. Soon my plate was piled high with delicacies, and I knew I couldn't eat it all. I would just have to eat what I could and hope no one noticed that I was wasting food. In my village, wasting food was frowned upon. You took only what you intended to eat.

We went back to our couches and rejoined Mago, Enidia, and Imilce. I made a brave attempt to consume what I had taken. Gisco said something to Imilce and she translated. "Gisco says he wants to fatten you up. Carthaginians like their women a little plump."

I smiled, pointed to my plate, and replied, "This will be a good start!" Imilce translated and everyone laughed. I looked up to see Hasdrubal the Fair, his wife Saponibal, and Hannibal coming toward us. Hannibal embraced Imilce and kissed her right there in public. That sort of open display of affection was not the custom in my village. Imilce did not seem to mind it, but I hoped that Gisco would not embarrass me in that way.

Imilce then introduced both Hasdrubal and Hannibal to me. Hasdrubal took my hand and kissed it. Imilce translated as he said, "It pleases me that your people and ours are now friends and allies, partners in our efforts to bring civilization and prosperity to Spain. I look forward to seeing you happily wed to my nephew Gisco." I didn't know what to say, so I just nodded. Then Hannibal in turn took my hand and kissed it. Something I saw in his eyes made me shiver. I clenched my teeth to gain control of my reaction. Hannibal was a strong, handsome, and powerful man. He was the kind of man that, ordinarily, I would be strongly attracted to. But I realized that the emotion that overwhelmed me wasn't lust; it was dread.

# TWO

## THE SIEGE OF SAGUNTUM

MAGO
KHART HADASHT, SPAIN, 219 B.C.

I, Mago Barca, am the youngest of Hamilcar Barca's three lion cubs. My brother Hannibal is five years older than I, and my brother Hasdrubal is three years older. Our father, Hamilcar Barca, was the best general Carthage produced in the twenty-three-year war against Rome. If we had had a few more like him we would have won that war. Father was not happy with the outcome of the war, and he inculcated in us, his sons, the notion that Rome is our enemy and that someday we must seek revenge for the injustices it has inflicted upon our nation.

My brother Hannibal journeyed to Spain with my father when he was nine years old. He grew up a child of the camp and trained in the arts of war from an early age. My brother Hasdrubal and I were educated in Carthage, but we each came to Spain when we reached eighteen. By the time we arrived our father was dead and Carthaginian Spain was ruled by our brother-in-law, Hasdrubal the Fair. I arrived in Spain with Gisco, my best friend since early childhood. He is the son of a wealthy neighbor, and is related on his mother's side to Hasdrubal the Fair. We had been educated together and had both decided upon military careers.

I had always worshiped my brother Hannibal from afar, as he left Carthage for Spain when I was five. Even when I came to Spain five years ago to join the Carthaginian army under our brother-in-law Hasdrubal the Fair, Hannibal and I never spent time alone together. As second in command he was constantly busy and constantly surrounded by underlings demanding his time. It came as a surprise when, shortly before our attack on Saguntum, he called me to his tent for a private conference. As I entered his tent I saw him seated at a small table poring over a map. There was a platter of bread and venison on the table, a bowl of fruit, a flask of wine, and two cups. He pointed toward the victuals and said "Help yourself, Mago." I nodded my thanks and took a small hunk of the meat and poured myself some wine.

"Mago," he said, "as you know, we will be taking on the Romans after we destroy Saguntum. I plan to take the army over the Alps, an arduous journey, and I think that the war will go on for several years. Are you with me on this? If you have any second thoughts, let me know now."

"Hannibal," I replied, "Why would you even ask me that question? You know I'm with you all the way on this. I am more than willing to die for our cause!"

"I ask this because it is my intention that you will be the most important person in the army after myself," said Hannibal. "You will be the key to my strategy to defeat the Romans in battle."

"What about Hasdrubal?" I asked

"I'm leaving Hasdrubal here in Spain to look after the province. It's entirely possible that the Romans will invade Spain to cut off our supply lines, and Hasdrubal must keep them open. He must also protect the silver mines, because the Romans will try to take them. He has a very important task ahead of him, but your mission is equally vital."

"So what will I be doing?" I asked.

"I'm assigning you to the command of a special group of soldiers, 5,000 men, made up of both Numidians and Spaniards, which will form the core of our ambush unit."

"Ambush unit?"

"Yes," said Hannibal, "The key to defeating the Romans in battle is surprise. I will be the one to choose the battlefields, and I will choose them with the intention of taking the Romans by surprise and keeping them off balance. If we can hide 5,000 foot soldiers and then send them in to attack the Roman flank once a battle is underway, we can cause such disruption in their lines that the battle will turn into a rout. Your job will be to lead these men, to train and discipline them so that they maintain complete silence, and no one moves until I give the signal. Do you think you are up to this task, Mago?"

"Yes," I said, "it's a great responsibility and I appreciate you trusting me with this. I won't fail you."

"I know you won't, Mago," said Hannibal.

"Gisco will be coming with us," I said. "I'd like to appoint him to be my lieutenant."

Hannibal frowned. "Do you really think Gisco has the makings of a soldier? I noticed he turned a bit green when he watched the crucifixion of our brother-in-law's assassin. He doesn't come from the same military background as we do. True, his grandfather was a general during the war with Rome, but his father is a merchant."

"He fought by my side at Arbocola, and he had no problem putting the defenders to the sword," I replied.

"Then I will trust your judgment," said Hannibal.

When we were children in Carthage, both my brother, Hasdrubal, and Gisco's brother Drubal thought Gisco simple. I suppose it was because he followed me everywhere and let me lead him into all sorts of mischief. We would raid the orchards of Megara, the wealthy suburb where we lived, and gorge on fruit; we would go into the inner city and see what we could steal from the stalls. We would pilfer an amphora of wine from one of our houses and drink it in secret. We always felt sick the next day but that didn't stop us from doing the same thing a few months later. Yes, he's always followed my lead and never seems to have had an original thought. But Gisco isn't stupid. I outshone him in martial arts and mathematics, but he far surpassed me in learning Greek and history. He's methodical and organized, and he's the one person I can rely upon to tell me the truth, even if I don't want to know the truth.

GISCO

About five months after the death of the assassin, Sansara gave birth to a daughter whom we named Giscana. I did not show my disappointment that she was not a boy. I stroked my wife's hair and whispered endearments to her. Even if she could not understand the endearments, she could sense their intent. Neither she nor I had desired this marriage, but she tried hard to please me and I had become fond of her. I knew that I would soon be leaving her, as Hannibal's plans for besieging Saguntum were proceeding apace. There was no point in castigating her for not having a boy, and I wanted her to remember me fondly.

Mago and I were both given the task of training and leading Spanish infantry. There were always rebellions breaking out among the tribes under Carthaginian rule, and we were kept busy putting them down. We confronted and defeated the Olcades, the Vaccaei, and the Carpetani. The latter were over 100,000 strong, but Hannibal prevailed against them by luring them across the river Tagus and setting our elephants and cavalry upon them as they were emerging from the stream. It was a great slaughter. After that we re-crossed the Tagus and set them to rout. Mago was right: Hannibal was full of tricks. I could only marvel at his genius. The defeat of the Carpetani gave Hannibal special satisfaction because this was the tribe that his father, Hamilcar Barca, died trying to subdue. Once we had subdued all the tribes of Spain, Hannibal was ready to deal with Saguntum.

By the time we set out for the siege of Saguntum we had over 100,000 in combined forces of Spaniards, Carthaginians, Numidians, Balearics, and Libyans. Owing to Mago's influence, I had been promoted to lieutenant and was now in Hannibal's inner circle. Hannibal called a meeting of his officers in his tent.

"We are about to lay siege to this wealthy city," Hannibal said. "We will surround its walls and let nothing and no one enter or leave. Our siege engines will batter the walls until they collapse.

When we conquer them, there will be rich rewards of booty and slaves shared among all who take part in this siege. I expect fierce resistance from the Saguntines, but in the end we will destroy them."

For a long moment no one spoke. Then my brother Drubal asked, "Do you think that the Romans will come to their aid?"

"They would be fools," said Hannibal, "and if they try, we are more than ready for them with 100,000 men at arms. In peacetime the Romans field only four legions of their own and four auxiliary legions from their allies—40,000 men. By the time they mobilize enough forces to confront us, Saguntum will be destroyed. This is not to say that the Romans won't declare war on Carthage over Saguntum, but when they do we will be ready for them and we will destroy them. It is my intention that Rome be permanently subjugated. In the long run there can be only one great power, and that must be Carthage.

"Maharbal," he continued, "you will lead the Numidian cavalry. Hasdrubal, my brother, you will take charge of the Spanish recruits from the Ilergites, the Seditani, and the Celtiberian tribes. Hasdrubal, son of Gisco, you will take charge of recruits from the southern tribes—the Lusitanians, the Turditani, the Volciani and so forth. Mago, you will take charge of the Balearics and the Libyans. Gisco, son of Gisco, you speak Greek, so I want you to supervise the siege engineers and the siege engines."

It was an important assignment for me, but a dangerous one because the top priority of the Saguntines would be to destroy the siege engines and anyone employed in their use.

The siege of Saguntum was a nightmare. The Saguntines had a weapon they called a *falarica*. It was a type of javelin with the shaft coated with pitch, which was set afire just before it was launched. The Saguntines made a sortie from their gates one afternoon and attacked our siege works, which had been battering their walls. One of them launched his falarica at me, and I tried to block it with my shield, but when it penetrated the shield it caught fire. The shield became too hot to handle and I had to drop it and fight unprotected. I drew my sword and shouted for my soldiers to counter-attack. Mago and I had trained together for warfare from an early age, and although he surpassed me in every skill, I was competent with a sword. Once our Saguntine assailants had launched their falaricas, they were defenseless before our swords. The Saguntines were bold and desperate, but they were not professional soldiers. The ground between the siege engine and the wall was soon littered with bodies, mostly Saguntine. Before we drove them off, however, they set fire to the *viniae*, which are covered walkways protecting the soldiers attempting to undermine the walls, and to the towers supporting the catapults. They also succeeded in killing one of the Greek engineers, as well several of my men who were manning the siege engines. I had to go to Hannibal and request increased protection. The catapults were useless for several days until we could construct new *viniae* and towers.

Hannibal was everywhere, cheering on the troops and supervising operations. Every day he inspected our efforts at breaking down the walls of the city. There were cracks in the thick walls and it was obvious that we were making progress. One day, however, he and his brother Hasdrubal came by late in the afternoon to assess the damage and they ventured too close to the wall. Suddenly I heard a loud cry. "Ahhh!" Hannibal lay on his back with a spear shaft protruding from his thigh. I shouted to my men, "Surround him with your shields!" We improvised a stretcher on the spot with planks and canvas from the viniae. Hannibal gritted his teeth in pain as we transferred him to the stretcher.

"Take him to his tent," shouted Hasdrubal. "Gisco, run and get that Greek physician, Eurycrates. Tell him it's an emergency."

I mounted a horse and rode to the medical tent where Eurycrates was supervising care of the wounded. He was in the middle of an amputation and the poor soldier was moaning with pain. "*Kyrios*,"

I said in Greek, "you need to come right away and bring your kit. Hannibal has been wounded in the thigh with a spear! He's been taken to his tent."

Eurycrates gave instructions to his assistants to finish the amputation. He gathered up his tools: knives, forceps, probes, and so forth; and cleaned them off with something that smelled like wine. He poured some concoction into a small flask and put it in his kit. Then he followed me to Hannibal's tent. He bent over Hannibal and examined the wound. Hannibal was still conscious and was breathing heavily, his eyes tightly shut.

"Bring lamps," he said, "all the lamps you can find. It's getting dark and I have to remove the spearhead. If we wait until tomorrow he will probably die. Give him this potion to drink; it is poppy juice and wine. It will lessen the pain. Then turn him on his side. I will need three people to hold him down so that he doesn't move when I extract the spearhead, two at his arms and one at his legs."

I gave Hannibal the potion to drink and in a few minutes his body seemed to relax. We aligned the lamps so the Eurycrates could get a good view of the wound. It took him only a few minutes to extract the spearhead, then he sewed the wound closed.

"It's fortunate that there was no damage to the bone," said Eurycrates, "it only penetrated the muscle."

Remembering the amputation I had just seen, I asked, "Kyrios, will the leg need to be amputated?"

"That depends," said the physician. "These wounds always become infected, but if there is white pus it is a sign that the body is fighting the infection. If the wound becomes blackened and vile smelling the infection will kill him unless the limb is amputated. We can only wait and hope."

All of Hannibal's officers gathered in Hasdrubal's tent to discuss the crisis. My brother asked, "What will we do if Hannibal dies, or remains too disabled to lead us?"

"I think Hannibal would have me take his place," said Hasdrubal.

"But would you be able to do the things that Hannibal has planned for us to do?" asked Mago. "Destroy Saguntum, then lead a large army over the Alps to Italy and destroy Rome?"

"We have tens of thousands of men who would follow Hannibal anywhere, even into Hades," said Hasdrubal Barca, "but I don't know if they would do the same for me. I don't think that any of us comes near to Hannibal in military genius, or in iron will and determination. I think that if our plans are to be realized, it must be Hannibal who leads us. If he dies or becomes disabled we must consider it a message from the gods that these things are not to be."

"Then would you have us abandon the siege and attempt to make peace with the Romans?" asked Mago.

"It may be too late to make peace with the Romans," said Hasdrubal Barca. "I would have us prepare to defend Spain. But we need not make any decisions until we know Hannibal's situation."

Within a week it became clear that Hannibal would survive, and that, with time, he would recover sufficiently from his wound to lead us. He had learned a valuable lesson and became more careful about his person.

Mago and I dined together once or twice a week. One evening we were eating a meal of wild pheasant that his slaves had hunted, and he told me, "Some ambassadors from Rome came to negotiate with Hannibal. He turned them away, telling them that he could not guarantee their safety and that he was too busy right now to see them. We think that they will be heading for Carthage now to complain to the Senate about the siege."

"What do you think the Senate will do?" I asked.

"Our faction is very strong now," said Mago. "I don't think they'll do anything to restrain us. Old Hanno's words will fall on deaf ears. He opposed making Hannibal commander in Spain. He's always hated our family, but most of the Senators side with us." He grinned. "After we conquer Saguntum, we'll have enough wealth to buy off almost any opposition. Hannibal thinks the Romans will declare war."

Then Mago startled me with a personal question. "How do you do it, Gisco?"

"Do what?"

"Handle women so well. You seem to get along so well with Sansara. I can't seem to get Enidia to warm up to me at all. In the bedroom she submits. It's as though it's a chore and she wants to get it done as quickly as possible."

I grinned. "I'm no expert on women. I can only say that they have their needs just as we have ours. We take our time in the bedroom, get to know each other as people and figure out what pleases the other. A little wine helps—not too much, mind you. It's part physical and part mental, and with a woman the mental comes before the physical—she wants to think that she's your queen, that she is the most important thing in the world to you, and I try to let her think that."

Mago sighed. "I would never be able to fool Enidia about that."

"And that's why your marriage will never satisfy either of you," I replied.

After more than seven months of siege, the Saguntines were getting more and more desperate. It became clear to them that there would be no succor from Rome. Two men escaped from the city and made their way to Hannibal to entreat him for terms to end the siege. Alcon was a citizen of Saguntum and Alorcus was a Spaniard. Hannibal permitted them to speak. Alcon spoke first. "We know that we can't hold out much longer. Is there no way that our city may be spared? Are there no terms that we might consider?"

Hannibal replied, "Your city, which has stubbornly held out for so long, must be destroyed. If your citizens wish their lives to be spared, they must agree to make restitution to the Turditani, and deliver up all of their gold and silver to us. Then they must depart from the city, each with a single garment, and settle in the place I appoint for them."

Alcon replied, "These terms are not acceptable. If I go back there and deliver them, I will be slain."

"These are my terms," said Hannibal. "The Saguntines must know that I will show no mercy if they do not accept them."

Alorcus, the Spaniard, said, "I will go back to Saguntum and deliver your terms. Surely they would prefer to preserve their lives, and not see their women ravished and their children sold into slavery."

He was wrong. The Saguntines refused the terms. They made a pyre of their gold and silver, and a number of them committed suicide by flinging themselves into the flames.

Soon after that, we made a breach in the walls with our siege engines, and Hannibal sent the whole of our forces into the city with instructions that all adult males be put to death. There was no other recourse, because the Saguntine men either shut themselves up with their wives and children and burned their houses over their own heads, or fought in the streets to the death. Our soldiers set about to plunder the city and to violate the women. I found that I had no appetite for either activity. The women would be scrawny and foul smelling and would probably bite and scratch, and as for plunder, I came from a very rich family and had always had a surfeit of material things, so I was content to leave pillage to the less affluent of our soldiers. Returning to our camp, I ran into my brother Drubal.

"What? Gisco, are you not going to avail yourself of the rights of the conqueror?" he asked.

"I prefer my women willing and clean," I said, "and I prefer my coupling relaxed and unhurried."

"I'm not so fastidious, Brother," he replied. "I'll take mine any way I can get it! What are you going to do when we conquer Rome? Just sit there and watch?"

I thought about this for a moment. "Rome has professionals, I'm told; women who know how to please men."

Drubal looked at me as if I were an idiot. "You'll pay for what you can get for free?"

"It's the quality, Brother, the quality." Drubal laughed and shook his head and went on his way to the conquered town. Although we were born of the same parents, Drubal and I were very different. We did not share the type of bond that united Hannibal and his brothers. I think the difficulties between us began with my birth. Uma nursed each of us herself, unlike mothers from other wealthy families who left the task to a wet nurse. Drubal was almost three when I was born and he was not happy when I replaced him at our mother's breast. He had resented me ever since. It did not help matters that I was comely in appearance and agreeable in personality. Drubal was ambitious and had an appetite for power. I, on the other hand, was always content to be a follower, and from a very young age, the person I followed everywhere was Mago. Mago, the youngest of Hamilcar Barca's lion cubs, was fearless and bold from an early age.

All the survivors of the siege were sold into slavery. I was given a number of slaves as booty, but I sold them all because I already had enough servants, and I knew that when spring came we would be embarking on our journey to Italia.

# THREE

## THE MARCH TO ITALIA

GISCO
218 B.C.

We wintered at Khart Hadasht. Hannibal gave all the Spanish troops leave to go home for the winter and told them to assemble here in the spring. He told them that we would be going on a campaign in foreign lands where there would be plenty of booty and opportunities for them to enrich themselves.

It was good to see Sansara and Giscana again. The baby was much changed. She had a full set of baby teeth now and a head of lush brown hair. She had started to walk, and her Phoenician-speaking nurse taught her to call me *Aba*. Sansara had picked up a few words here and there but we still couldn't carry on a conversation. At least I'll be able to talk to Giscana someday, I thought. That is, if I ever see her again after we leave for Italia.

My brother and I got permission to sail to Carthage to see our parents. I brought Sansara and Giscana along so that my parents could see their granddaughter. Living with my Aba and Uma were Drubal's Carthaginian wife, Amashtar, and their two children, Caphonbal and Bomilcar, aged four and two respectively, as well as Buba, my father's aged mother. Buba was a widow. Her husband, my grandfather Gisco, had been a general during the war with Rome and had died a horrible death at the hands of the mercenaries during the uprising that had followed that war. Buba said, "Why did you marry a Spanish woman who can't even speak to you?"

"It's political, Buba," I said. "Hasdrubal the Fair asked me to marry her so he could make an alliance with her tribe."

"Pah!" proclaimed Buba. "I've never heard of anything so ridiculous!"

Aba and Uma just smiled. Old people don't understand these things. Aba and Uma considered Sansara beneath me, but it was something that couldn't be helped. They adored their granddaughter Giscana. We stayed in Carthage for a month, and I bought Sansara a lot of nice clothes and jewelry. We ate and drank lavishly the whole time. I thought of leaving her and Giscana with my parents but decided that she would be better off in Spain, where at least there were women she could talk to.

## SANSARA

Gisco has left me to follow Mago and Hannibal to Italia to make war on the Romans. Before he left we paid a visit to his native city, Carthage. If I thought Khart Hadasht was magnificent, it is nothing compared to the splendor of old Carthage. It's a huge city with hundreds of thousands of inhabitants. The ordinary people there live in concrete buildings six stories high. It is a city of merchants and they trade with every nation in the world. I could not believe the things I saw for sale in the markets. I could have spent hours watching a craftsman blowing glass into the shapes of animals. There were shops specializing in jewelry where you could find every kind of precious stone. My eye caught a piece of amber set in a pendant. It actually had a fly in it that had been trapped during its formation. Gisco said that amber comes from the forests of northern Europe and finds its way to Carthage by trade. It is rare and precious. There were shops that sold carpets and wall hangings. I asked Gisco if I could purchase some for our quarters. Other shops sold robes in every conceivable color and design, and Gisco bought several for me to take home to Khart Hadasht. There were also places that sold artwork, statues, and idols. There were others that specialized in spices. There were even some that sold children's toys. I bought Giscana a doll. There was so much to see and so little time to see it.

Gisco's father, also called Gisco, lives in a mansion in a part of the city they call Megara. All the rich people live there to escape the noise and bustle of the city. Megara is very beautiful, with streams and orchards and all kinds of lush vegetation. Birds and other wildlife are abundant. Their mansion is two stories high and contains several apartments and a servant's quarters. There is a spacious dining hall where the family gathers for meals, and a bath house similar to the one in the palace in Khart Hadasht.

I am beginning to understand a little bit of Phoenician but I couldn't really follow the conversation at the table. I can say such phrases as "The food is good," and "thank you, but I don't want any more," and that sort of thing. Gisco's father and mother were kind and patient with me. They showered Giscana with toys and baby clothes.

Gisco's niece Caphonbal and nephew Bomilcar like to play with Giscana. She is walking now and they let her play with their toys. Their mother, Amashtar, doesn't seem very friendly. She hardly talks to me at all and pays no attention to Giscana.

After a month we sailed back to Khart Hadasht. It was around the time of the summer solstice that Gisco told me he was leaving. We were in bed and had just made love. "I want you to wait for me," he said. "Do you understand?" I nodded, fighting back tears. "If I die in battle, my family will take care of you and Giscana. I have made arrangements with my father. If I survive, I will come back to you. I think this war will last for two or three years, but I want you to wait for me. I love you and Giscana."

"Yes," I said. "I will wait. Come back to me, Gisco. I love you."

It has been two months since Gisco left and I wonder where he is and how he is doing. I have not had my courses for these two months and I think I may be with child.

## MAGO

Gisco and I accompanied Hannibal to Gades where he sacrificed to the god Melquart so that our enterprises might prosper. Gades is a Phoenician city far older than Khart Hadasht, possibly even older than old Carthage. Its temples and idols are venerated by all peoples of Phoenician descent.

In the spring the Spanish recruits returned from their leaves of absence and we began to prepare for our journey. Hannibal left behind our brother, Hasdrubal, with a large number of infantry and cavalry to protect our interests in Spain in case the Romans should invade. He sent a force of Spanish soldiers along with Gisco's brother Drubal to Africa to protect the territories of Carthage in case the Romans should invade or the tribes under our rule rebel.

We proceeded by forced marches northward and crossed the Iberus. I was surprised to see Sosylus, our Greek teacher, on the march with us. "Sosylus," I said, "you're coming with us all the way to Italia? Aren't you a bit too old for this sort of journey?"

"Well, I am a Spartan, after all," he smiled. "We're a hardy lot. This expedition promises to be a momentous event in the history of the world, and I plan to write about it."

There were 90,000 infantry and 12,000 cavalry who crossed the Iberus. We were attacked by the Ilergetes, the Bargusii, and the Ausetani, but they were quickly subdued. Hannibal permitted the departure of 7,000 Spanish troops who did not want to leave Spain, and he left ten thousand infantry and 1,000 cavalry with Hanno for the defense of northern Spain. That left 73,000 infantry and 11,000 cavalry to start across the Pyrenees. We also brought along 37 elephants. Years ago King Pyrrhus of Epirus disconcerted the Romans with his elephants and Hannibal thought that they might once again be effective against the Roman legions.

I walked alongside Gisco and Sosylus. "Hannibal told me about a dream he had the other night," I told them.

"What sort of dream?" asked Sosylus.

"He said that he had seen the vision of a divine youth who told him he was there to guide him to Italia," I said. "The youth told him that he must follow him and not look back. For some reason Hannibal could not resist looking back, and when he did he beheld a huge serpent that was wreaking tremendous destruction of trees and bushes and was followed by a mass of thunderclouds."

"What do you think the vision meant?" asked Sosylus.

"The youth told Hannibal that the vision represented the devastation of Italia that he would bring in his wake," I said. "He told him that he should advance forward and not inquire further."

"That must mean that we will wreak havoc when we get to Italia," Said Gisco.

"If I know Hannibal," I said, "I'm sure we will."

"Perhaps your father Hamilcar will hear of it in the netherworld," said Sosylus. "He'll be proud of his sons."

We crossed the Pyrenees without great hardship. We saw snow on the mountain peaks but our trail did not rise to that elevation. When we reached Gallia we made camp in Illiberis. Hannibal conferred with various Gallic leaders and gave them presents of gold and silver in exchange for allowing our safe passage through their territories. In a few days we reached the Rhone River. The river was hundreds of feet wide, a formidable barrier. Hannibal, Bomilcar, Maharbal, Sosylus, Gisco, and I gathered at the west bank and looked out over the expanse.

"What do you think, Mago?" Hannibal asked me.

"I see three problems, Hannibal," I said. "How to get the men across, how to get the elephants across, and what to do about the hostile Volcae tribesmen waiting for us on the other side."

"Very good, Mago," said Hannibal, "any suggestions?"

"We can purchase watercraft from the locals or make our own," I said. "Perhaps we could construct a bridge for the elephants."

"I was thinking more in terms of rafts for the elephants," said Hannibal. "We could construct platforms fifty feet wide and 200 feet long, and cover them with earth so that the beasts think that they are still traveling on land. Then we construct similar rafts of fifty feet wide and 100 feet long and attach them to ends of the first rafts. When the elephants cross over to the second raft we detach it from the first and convey the beasts to the other side," said Hannibal. "But first, as you say, we have to deal with the Volcae."

Hannibal turned to Bomilcar. "Bomilcar, I am having the men hollow out canoes as the local tribesmen have shown us. I want you to take 1,000 men across the river, but cross it at a point several miles upstream. When you have reached the other side, send up smoke signals so that we know where you are. Then wait for my signal. I will send our forces across the river, and at the same time you march south and attack the Volcae in the rear."

Over the next several days the crafts were built and Bomilcar's force crossed to the other side. The plan worked to perfection— the Volcae, seeing that they were outflanked, fled, and we were able to establish a secure camp on the east bank. On the west bank the men set about building the rafts to be used for the transport of the elephants. There were a few cases in which an elephant panicked and plunged into the water, but these ended up swimming to the shore and were recaptured.

It was here that we encountered our first Romans. The Roman Consul Publius Cornelius Scipio had arrived in southern Gallia and had sent out a band of cavalry for reconnaissance. Hannibal had also sent out a band of Numidian cavalry for a similar purpose. Our two bands met and began fighting. We lost some 200 cavalrymen while the Romans lost a similar number. Maharbal returned with the surviving Numidians and reported the encounter to Hannibal.

"Our scouts have reported that Scipio's camp is thirty stadia to the south of here," said Maharbal. "Are we going to do battle with him?"

"No," said Hannibal. "I don't want to delay our crossing of the Alps. The longer we delay the worse the weather will be."

We undertook a series of forced marches eastward toward the Alps. By the time Scipio discovered where our camp had been, we were long gone.

"Do you really think we're adequately equipped for crossing the Alps?" Gisco asked me. "I've heard it gets exceedingly cold up there."

"Hannibal plans to obtain supplies of furs and footwear from the Allobroges," I said. "The Gauls wear britches for a reason and I think that we will just have to get used to them, at least until we reach a warmer climate." Indeed, Hannibal settled a quarrel between two princes of the Allobroges in favor of Brancus, the elder, and the tribesmen assisted us with obtaining the necessary supplies of food and clothing.

The thought of crossing the Alps was daunting, and there were a number of desertions. Hannibal assembled our troops and spoke on the subject of crossing the Alps. "Soldiers," he said, "you know that no part of the earth reaches the sky, and there is no place on earth that is insurmountable by mankind. These Alps are inhabited and cultivated. Men, women, and children have been crossing the Alps for centuries. You see before you Boii tribesmen who have just crossed the Alps from Italia. Let us proceed with confidence because great rewards await us in Italia!"[1]

---

[1]   Ab Urbe Condita by Titus Livius. Book XXI.30

## GISCO

I have to confess that the two weeks we spent crossing the Alps were the most harrowing and arduous of my life, as well as the most frigid! I would rather fight in ten pitched battles than ever make that journey again! What was Hannibal thinking? We were Carthaginians, Numidians, and Spaniards. We have lived only in the warm climates of Africa and southern Spain. None of us were accustomed to long marches in snow! I didn't know what was worse: the long, arduous, and exhausting days, or the long frigid nights! I recall that I was amazed when I woke up one morning and could actually see my breath. For the first few minutes it was amusing to watch the white clouds come out of our mouths. It never got cold enough to see your own breath in Carthage or in southern Spain. Then, a few days later, our march took us into the snow. I had never seen snow up close before. It blanketed the landscape. I would have admired the beauty of it if it hadn't been so accursedly cold.

On the third day of our climb we heard shouts and screams ahead of us. A messenger ran down the line toward us. "Stop! Don't go any farther! They're hurling boulders down at us!" We stopped in our tracks. It was merely a matter of chance which man or beast would be struck and go hurtling to his death.

"Who are these people?" I asked.

"I think they might be rebel Allobroges, unhappy with Hannibal's support of their chieftain Brancus," said Sosylus.

Toward evening Hannibal called us to a meeting around his campfire. Our army had been split in two, some having run the gantlet of the boulders and passed to the east.

"My scouts tell me that the tribesmen do not stay up on the ledges at night but go home to their villages," said Hannibal. "Mago, Bomilcar, Gisco, Monomachus, Maharbal, and Hanno, I want each of you take a dozen men and occupy each of the six ledges to the east of here. When the barbarians come back in the morning, kill as many as you can."

Before dawn I marched my team to the third of the ledges. Marching in darkness, in extreme cold, and with the wind in our faces was not easy, but we reached our ledge and when the sun rose we were there waiting for them. I'll never forget the expressions on the barbarian's faces when they arrived and encountered a dozen heavily armed soldiers on their ledges. They hadn't even bothered to approach in stealth. I threw my javelin at a tall, blond, robust man who appeared to be their leader, striking him in the neck. He tumbled backward. I wasn't sure whether I had killed him, so I took the precaution of plunging my sword into his heart. I was immediately assaulted by a screaming man whom I guessed might be the leader's son. He was only armed with a spear, which I easily dodged. I put him to the sword. We killed as many as we could, but most of them fled precipitously.

Hannibal ordered us to pillage and burn one of their larger villages to teach them a lesson. When we got to the village the inhabitants had fled, but we found a crippled old crone and made her tell us where their grain was stored. I heard a voice call my name. "Rab Gisco!" I saw no one but when I entered the lodge where I thought the voice came from there were six of our men bound to posts by leather thongs. The barbarians had taken them prisoner. I recognized them as Mago's Spanish recruits whom I had helped train. The man who had recognized me was named Lucos. He had seen us through a slit in the wall.

"Rab Gisco," he said "Thank Turovex you've come! They would have killed us or sold us as slaves!" Turovex was one of their gods. I took out my knife and cut their bonds.

"Can you walk?" I asked. "Can you make it back to the camp?" The six rose unsteadily to their feet.

"I think we just need to get the blood flowing to our legs," said Lucos. "Any food?"

My men and I shared bread from our packs with the freed prisoners. After setting fire to all of the barbarians' dwellings, we started back to the camp with our booty.

We marched on, day after day, climbing higher and higher. I found myself struggling for breath. Sosylus said that at these altitudes the air is thin. Sometimes the cold wind blew in our faces and made our progress very slow. At night we constructed a windbreak and huddled around a fire eating our meager rations. One evening we were gathered around our campfire and Monomachus came up with what he thought was a perfect solution to our food shortage.

"There are plenty of dead bodies along the trail and the cold keeps them from spoiling. Certainly they would provide us with food for the rest of our journey!" Monomachus was an ugly, burly beast of a man. Whenever Hannibal wanted a particularly abhorrent task performed, he left it to Monomachus.

I exclaimed "Monomachus! You would have us eat our dead comrades? Men we've known and marched with all these months? Men who perished in our cause?" I was ready to draw my sword.

Hannibal interceded, "Monomachus, we don't eat our brothers. If an elephant or a horse dies, by all means, eat it. We will survive without resorting to your plan. I don't want Sosylus to record that we were cannibals."

The only person who seemed cheerful was Sosylus. He consistently appeared calm and tranquil. He must have been well into his forties, his beard streaked with gray. In the evenings he would share the campfire with us and, as we listened to the howling wind outside our lean-to, he would regale us with tales of the ancient heroes of Greece. Spartans are reputed to be men of few words, but Sosylus was full of chatter. He knew the Iliad and the Odyssey by heart and would quote from one or the other at length. One night he related the story of the battle of Marathon, in which the Athenians had vanquished an army of Persians more than three times their size nearly 300 years ago. "Have you told this story to Hannibal?" Mago asked.

"Certainly," said Sosylus. "And Hannibal plans to use their strategy against the Romans. He will have to, since we will be facing armies far larger than ours." I think that if Sosylus had not been there to divert us and set an example of cheerful endurance of extreme hardship, I never would have survived this ordeal.

The worst part of the journey was the descent from the summit. It was so steep and slippery that we had to walk sideways to avoid falling. At one point we were stopped by a wall of rock left by an avalanche. We had to carve a passage through the rock using heated vinegar to soften the rock so that it would crumble to our axes. It took us four days to make a passage wide enough for the elephants. Finally we looked out over a green and fertile valley where we could send our starving beasts out to pasture.

"Italia!" exclaimed Mago, looking out over the expanse. "Ours for the taking!"

Our journey had been a brutal ordeal with major losses. Hannibal estimated that between raids by the mountain dwellers, mishaps in climbing, exposure, and disease, we lost 36,000 men during the passage. Given the desertions that took place before we entered the Alps, we probably numbered about 40,000, of whom there were some 30,000 infantry and 10,000 cavalry. At least half of the elephants had died, and those that remained were not in very good condition.

# FOUR

## TICINUS, TREBIA, AND TRASIMENE

### HANNIBAL'S FIRST VICTORIES

MAGO
218–217 B.C.

Hannibal set about trying to make alliances with the Gallic tribes. We entered Italia through the land of the Insubrians, who hated the Romans and were well disposed to our cause. The Insubrians were at war with the Taurini, and when Hannibal tried to make an alliance with the Taurini, they proved hostile. To make an example of this tribe Hannibal ordered a siege of their capital, Taurinorum. We destroyed the entire city, killing all of the inhabitants. The plunder kept us fed for a time. Hannibal wanted to make it clear to the Gallic tribesmen of northern Italia that they had two choices: They could make an alliance with us and give us food and assistance, or they could refuse to make an alliance with us and see their towns destroyed and their lands despoiled. If they did not give willingly, we would take what we needed by force.

During this time we had taken a number of Gallic prisoners and kept them in chains. Hannibal assembled them and shouted, "Who among you desires liberty?"

This was translated and each of the prisoners shouted, "I!" in his own language.

"We will choose pairs by lot. You will fight to the death. The victor will be freed, awarded armor and a horse. The vanquished will be freed from his misery."

Those who were chosen danced with joy. We watched as each pair fought to the death, and the victor was praised for his strength and skill, while the vanquished was praised no less for dying bravely. True to his word, Hannibal gave the victor in each contest a horse and a set of armor and each rode off proudly to the cheers and applause of his countrymen.

Hannibal then gave a speech in which he held these men up as examples.

"Soldiers, you have seen how these men fought bravely for their lives," he said. "Some were victorious and survived; others died, but are no longer in chains. We are now in the same situation as these men," he said. "We must either be victorious, or die. If we are victorious all who survive will receive tax-free land in Africa, Spain, or Italia, and any who desire it will receive Carthaginian citizenship."[2]

The Roman Consul, Publius Cornelius Scipio, had departed from his army in Gaul and had sent his soldiers to northern Spain with his brother Gneius Cornelius Scipio. Having returned to Italia by ship, he now commanded two legions of relatively raw recruits and was camped on the other side of the Ticinus River. He had about 7,000 infantry and 3,500 cavalry. I did not take part in the battle, as Hannibal used only the cavalry, which numbered

---

[2]    Ibid Book XXI.45

about 6,000. Hannibal ordered a charge and our cavalry scattered and routed the Roman infantry and inflicted severe damage on their cavalry. Gisco, Sosylus, and I watched the scene from a hill. We caught sight of Scipio, the Roman commander, in his red cloak. He was struck by a javelin and fell from his horse. His bodyguard surrounded him to protect him but, one by one, they were overcome.

"Look at that crazy fool!" cried Gisco. Unexpectedly a rider came charging down from the hill opposite to where we were standing, followed by about thirty others. They dispersed our soldiers, who were closing in on the Consul and, with some assistance from his men, their leader picked up the Consul, put him on his horse and rode toward safety.

"By Melqart, we've been cheated!" I shouted.

"But I've never seen anything quite so daring and spectacular!" said Sosylus. "Who was that Roman soldier leading the charge? He deserves a place in my history for that deed!"

We couldn't help but admire the audacity of the man who led the rescue party. Only much later would we learn that the man was the Consul's son, of the same name, only seventeen years old, Publius Cornelius Scipio the Younger. Had this youth been killed in his hazardous and daring charge to rescue his father, the whole war might have turned out very differently.

Victory was clearly ours. We had killed over 2,000 Romans with minimal casualties on our part. Hannibal sent the Numidian cavalry after the survivors. Unfortunately, the Numidians devoted too much time to pillaging Scipio's abandoned camp, and Scipio's army was able to cross the bridge over the Ticinus, then dismantle the bridge to delay our forces. Scipio made his way to the relative safety of Placentia.

The next day we were joined by 2,200 Gallic soldiers, who had deserted from Scipio. Their leader proclaimed "We greet you, noble Hannibal, and we bear gifts that will please you!"

The gifts were severed heads of Romans that they had taken when they had attacked one of their camps. Hannibal considered this a good omen. The Gauls, long oppressed by Rome, would come over to our side now that they saw that we could easily out-fight the Romans. After all, what choice did they have? If Rome could not protect them from us, they would be wise to join us. Hannibal sent the Gauls off to try to persuade their tribesmen to ally with us.

## GISCO

Hunger began to gnaw at our bellies. Winter was approaching and there was little to forage. Hannibal learned of the existence of a granary in Clastidium. He sent Mago and me to negotiate with the commander of the garrison there. We approached under a flag of truce. There were two sentries at the town gate.

"Who goes there?" demanded one of them.

"Does anyone here speak Greek?" I asked.

The man looked befuddled. He sent his companion to fetch the commanding officer. A portly man in the uniform of a Roman military tribune emerged from the gate. I asked him if he spoke Greek.

"Yes," he said. "I am from Brundisium, which was settled centuries ago by Greeks. My name is Dasius. What do you want? What are you doing here?"

I translated Mago's words. "You have grain, and our army needs this grain. We could take this town by force, but Hannibal would prefer to save our efforts for more important matters. How much money would it take for you to peacefully surrender this town and its granary if we guarantee that none of your soldiers or townspeople will be harmed?"

"Do I understand this correctly?" asked Dasius. "You want me to surrender our granary to you. If I do, I will be paid, and our soldiers and townspeople will not be harmed. If I don't, you will attack the town, take it by force, kill our soldiers, and enslave the townspeople?"

I translated this for Mago. "Tell him he understands perfectly," replied Mago. "Except that we will not enslave the townspeople. We will kill them all. This is what we did in Taurinorum when they refused to cooperate with us."

"I see," said Dasius. "Give me 400 gold pieces and the town and granary are yours."

We reported our success to Hannibal and he returned with us to firm up our agreement with Dasius. Dasius invited our delegation to a meal and we sat on couches in his dining hall while his servants brought us dishes of fowl, bread, cheese and olives, and fruits and vegetables. The food, although plain, was much tastier than anything I'd had since leaving Khart Hadasht. I began to pine for the comforts of civilization.

"Lieutenant Gisco says that you are from Brundisium, Dasius," said Hannibal. "Where in Italia is that?"

"It's in Apulia, on the Adriatic coast," replied Dasius.

"And the people of Apulia," asked Hannibal, "how do they feel about the Romans?"

Dasius seemed to weigh his answer carefully. "The Romans are tolerated but not loved. We are subjects but not citizens."

"I have come to Italia to subdue the Romans and release Italia from their grasp," said Hannibal. "Is there a chance that the people of Apulia might welcome liberation from Rome?"

"Yes, there's a chance," Said Dasius, "If you approach them in the spirit of a liberator rather than a conqueror. Perhaps I may be of assistance. I will join you if you will have me. Obviously I will not be able to return to the service of Rome. I speak both Greek and Latin and I know how to command men."

"We will be pleased to have you in our service, Dasius," replied Hannibal.

I was amazed that someone could so easily become a traitor, but then I reflected that Dasius was not really a Roman and had little loyalty to Rome. I believed that I could not betray Carthage under any circumstances. I could not then imagine how circumstances might prove me wrong.

We kept our bargain and he kept his. The grain from Clastidium kept our army fed for the winter.

The wounded Consul, Scipio, did not seem eager to do battle with us. A few weeks after his defeat at the river Ticinus, however, he was joined by the other Consul. It seems that in Rome the highest office is shared by two men, as it is in Carthage. The difference between Rome and Carthage is that Roman Consuls go out into the field and lead troops, which are levied from among the citizens. In Carthage the leadership of the military is left up to professional soldiers, and most of the troops are mercenaries. This gives Carthage the advantage of having well-trained and seasoned troops, while the Roman troops are, for the most part, ill trained and untried. The Roman Consuls are not always good generals, and Scipio's co-Consul, a man named Tiberius Sempronius Longus, was especially incompetent.

Hannibal called a meeting of his officers. "Mago, I want you and Gisco to take 1,000 foot soldiers and 1,000 cavalry and hide yourselves in the swampland between the river and our camp. Tomorrow morning I will send Maharbal with his Numidians across the river to raid the Roman camp. They will harass the Romans, inflict a few casualties, and then withdraw across the river. Remember what we did with the Carpetani? If Sempronius is as stupid as I think he is, he will send his forces across the river to assault our camp, and you will be waiting in ambush."

Mago grinned. "My first chance to kill actual Romans! This will be a treat!"

We were camped on the left bank of the river Trebia while Sempronius made his camp on the right. It was around the time of the winter solstice, so the Trebia was icy cold. Hannibal sent the Numidian cavalry across the river early in the morning to harass the Romans in their camp. After a time the Numidians withdrew across the river. Sempronius, every bit as stupid as Hannibal thought him to be, then gathered up his unfed troops and sent both infantry and cavalry across the river. The cavalry were not greatly affected by the cold, but the infantry, having forded the river through icy water up to their chests, could scarcely wield their weapons. They were easy prey for our ambush. It was my first time to shed Roman blood and I killed dozens of them with my sword. It seemed a pity that they were too debilitated from the cold to put up much of a fight, but I think that it was a great measure of Hannibal's genius that he arranged conditions of battle so that it was so easy to kill Romans. In none of the three battles I fought in under Hannibal's standard in Italia did I feel my life to be at great risk. This would certainly not be the case in later years when I fought under the standards of Hasdrubal Barca, Mago Barca or my brother Drubal. And it would not be the case at the battle of Zama when Hannibal had a much debilitated army and the Romans had produced their own military genius, Publius Cornelius Scipio Africanus.

The battle was not quite as one-sided as that of the Ticinus, because the Roman cavalry inflicted about 5,000 fatalities on our infantry; but the Romans lost close to 30,000 men by the end of the day, over two-thirds of their forces. Sempronius managed to escape with most of his cavalry to Placentia.

Despite our two significant victories, we continued to experience hardship. Winters are harsh in northern Italia, and there was an ice storm that destroyed our tents. This was followed by a cold snap in which all but one of our remaining elephants died. We survived for the next three months on the grain that we had obtained in Clastidium.

## MAGO

What a glorious day this was! I finally had a chance to slay Romans and to prove to my brother Hannibal that he had been wise to assign me to the command of the ambush squad!

Last night Hannibal called me to his tent and told me to instruct my men to rise before dawn, eat quickly and arm themselves. I was to take them to hide in the marsh north of the River Trebia.

"How do you know the Romans will cross the river and attack?" I asked him.

"I'm going to provoke them," Said Hannibal, "my spies tell me that Sempronius is angry at what we have been doing in this region, all the pillaging, burning, and destroying farms. I don't think it will take much provocation. He is said to be a man who acts rashly."

My brother was right. Before mid-morning the Romans were crossing the icy Trebia. We remained in hiding until all their infantry was across, then Hannibal gave the signal and we attacked them on their left flank, while they were engaged with our infantry on their front, and with our elephants and cavalry on their right. The Roman foot soldiers were weakened by having to wade through the icy water of the Trebia, and by not having had breakfast. They fought as well as they could in their sorry condition. Romans do not give up easily. The combat was at close quarters, mostly with swords. The Romans had an advantage over my Spanish and African foot soldiers in that they had better armor. Many wore chain mail and breast plates; their shields were large and strong, with a boss in the middle that could be used to ram an enemy. Their helmets provided protection for the head and most of the neck. The armor, however, came at a cost to mobility. I instructed my soldiers to thrust to the front of the neck if possible, the most vulnerable part of the well-armed Roman legionary.

Even under these nearly ideal conditions of combat, with a physically weakened enemy, the attack was not without risk, and, while this day was the best day of my life so far, it was also the day that I came closest to losing my life. As I was attacking one of the Romans, maneuvering so that I could make the killing thrust, another came at me and knocked me off balance with his shield. I fell to the ground and rolled out of the way just as he brought his sword down. His sword missed me by a finger's breadth. But now both my original target and his friend closed in on me. There was no way that I could kill both of them before one of them killed me. Gisco solved my problem by slicing off the second man's sword arm, and then delivering the fatal thrust to the neck, while I dispatched my original target. Gisco had saved my life, but there was no time to thank him. We were both immediately assaulted by furious Roman swordsmen.

My men had seen the confrontation and they were determined to protect me. They surrounded me and fended off further attacks. They concentrated their forces so that every time a Roman came near me they killed him before he could get to me. It was embarrassing, but I could see their point of view. Hannibal would not be happy with them if they allowed me to be slain. Gisco had no such protection and continued to slay Romans with complete abandon. I later asked him how many he had killed and he shook his head. "I have no idea," he said.

SANSARA
KHART HADASHT, 217 B.C., MARCH

I have just given birth to a beautiful baby boy. I have named him Gisco after his father. It is such a wondrous thing to see a new little person emerge from your body, despite the pain involved. I love the feel of his mouth sucking at my breast. I love looking at his little face. He will look just like his father, I think. He has Gisco's dimples when he smiles.

Gisco has been gone for nine months and my nights are lonely without him. Giscana is beginning to talk, and she prefers to talk to me in Phoenician, which her nursemaid has taught her.

Imilce came to see me yesterday to congratulate me about the baby.

"What a beautiful baby!" she exclaimed. "Look at those dimples, and all that hair! Looks just like his Aba!

"We've received word about the expedition to Italia," she continued. "Hannibal sent a long dispatch and Hasdrubal read it to Saponibal. She told us that Hannibal won a big victory over the Romans at the end of last year. He's recruited a lot of the Celtic tribesmen, who hate the Romans. Hannibal plans to march on Rome. Both Mago and Gisco are alive and well."

"Ah, thank the gods!" I said. "Enidia must be happy too!"

"No, I think Enidia doesn't care a thing for Mago. She's not happy here and wants to go home to her village. What about you, Sansara?"

"I miss my mother and my friends, but I promised Gisco I would wait for him. I think he will be happy that he has a son. And it would be hard for me to go back to living in a primitive village after living these past three years in Khart Hadasht." We both laughed.

"I wish I could write to Mother and tell her about her grandchildren," I said, "but I don't know how to write and no one in my village knows how to read."

"Saponibal is going back to Carthage," said Imilce. "Things will be more relaxed around here when she's not around to poke her nose into everyone's business. Maybe next summer we could ask Hasdrubal if we could have an escort and make an expedition to your village. We could drop Enidia off at her village, and on the way back, you and I could visit Castulo and I could see my parents."

"Oh, Imilce! I would be so happy if you could make that happen!" I exclaimed.

Imilce is such a beautiful and kind person. There is really no point in revealing to her my loathing for her husband. I'm not even sure myself why I hate him. Perhaps it's because he took Gisco away from me. But no, I hated him before that. I hated him from the moment I met him. There's nothing personal about it. He has always treated me with due respect. It's just that he seems to me the incarnation of evil. He is obsessed with vengeance against the Romans, and he'll destroy everything in his path to satisfy this obsession. Multitudes will die before he completes his task. And my beloved Gisco follows him blindly.

# GISCO

When spring came Hannibal decided to bring us to Etruria. For four days and three nights we marched through a swamp. Now that's another thing I swear I'll never do again! It was almost as bad as crossing the Alps! I was with Mago in the rear. The task of the rear guard was to dissuade the Gauls from deserting. The Gauls are bold and fierce, but they lack stamina. There was no place to rest except on the backs of dead animals or abandoned packs. Hannibal rode on the back of Sirius, our one remaining elephant. Unfortunately, Hannibal contracted an eye infection and lost the sight in one of his eyes. We finally emerged from the swamp not far from Arretium, where the new Roman Consul Gaius Flaminius had his camp. Hannibal's orders were for us to lay waste to the countryside in hopes of getting Flaminius to engage us in a pitched battle. The battle of Trebia had taken place on the winter solstice; this next battle would take place on the summer solstice.

It seems that solstices are not auspicious for the Romans! When we reached Lake Trasimene, Hannibal deployed his forces all along the defile between the mountains and the lake in readiness for the ambush. I was with the African and Spanish troops on the hill at the eastern side of the valley. The Balearic slingers and pike men were posted at the right end of the valley and the Gauls and cavalry occupied the left end of the valley. Flaminius and his men had no idea what awaited them.

When Flaminius marched his men into the defile along the lake, the fog was so thick that they could scarcely see ten feet in front of themselves. We waited until all of them had come into our trap and then we attacked. It was a slaughter. The Romans had nowhere to run except into the lake, and if they did that, their heavy armor caused them to drown. It is believed that we killed 15,000 Romans that day. The Consul, Flaminius, was said to have been killed by one of our allied Gallic chieftains, a man named Ducarius. It was sweet revenge for an attack on his tribe that the

Consul had made some years before. Flaminius's body was never found. He was the first Roman Consul to die at the hands of our army, but he would not be the last.

There was a vanguard of Roman cavalry, some 6,000 men, who fought their way through our ranks and took refuge in an Etruscan village. The next day Hannibal sent Maharbal and his Numidian cavalry to hunt them down. Maharbal surrounded the village and told their military tribune through an interpreter that if they surrendered they would be released with only a single garment. The group agreed to surrender and delivered up their weapons, armor, and horses. Maharbal then herded them back to our camp.

"Maharbal," said Hannibal, "I did not authorize you to make a deal with the Romans. If we release them we will have to fight these same men again in the near future, and they are trained cavalrymen who present the greatest threat to our army. We have to eliminate these men as a threat. I have been in contact with Greek slave traders who work both sides of the Adriatic. We'll profit from the sale of these captives. I may consider releasing those who are from tribes allied with the Romans. They may be persuaded to go to their people and convince them to ally with us. But the Romans must be sold as slaves."

"I am sorry, Hannibal," said Maharbal. "Now that you have explained your reasoning, I must agree. I won't do this again."

I was assigned to supervise the handling of the prisoners. I had my men put them in chains. We had little food to spare, so they got only a meager bowl of porridge a day. They were a sullen-looking lot, but then I suppose I would also be sullen if I were in their situation. Sosylus wandered around the compound taking notes. "That boy looks too young to be a soldier." He said to me, indicating a beardless youth. "I wonder if I might talk to him." I suspected that Sosylus might have an erotic interest in the comely young man. Neither Phoenicians nor Romans approve of erotic relations between men, but it seems that the Greeks, in general, and Spartans, in particular, have no problem with it. I have heard that Spartan boys, upon reaching the age of puberty, routinely acquire an adult lover, and Spartan women, upon their nuptials, cut their hair short and dress like boys in order to arouse their new husbands. I looked on with amusement as Sosylus approached the young man.

He smiled. "*Ephebos*, do you speak Greek?"

The boy looked surprised but said, "Yes."

"You seem young to be in the Roman cavalry. How old are you?" asked Sosylus.

"I'm seventeen," replied the boy.

"I'm amazed that such an inexperienced soldier as you could have survived this battle! How did you do it?"

The boy shrugged. "I rode through the enemy lines and whenever anyone attacked me I killed them with my sword. What else could I do? Who are you and why do you ask?"

"I'm Sosylus of Sparta," said Sosylus. "I plan to write a history of this war. You speak Greek very well. Who taught you?"

"My teacher was Livius Andronicus," replied the young man.

"Livius Andronicus the playwright?" asked Sosylus.

"Yes," said the boy. "My father was a client of Tiberius Servilius Livius, who was Andronicus's patron, and I was allowed to study with him along with Livius's sons.

"And what is your name?" asked Sosylus.

"Enneus Tullius," the boy replied.

"Well, Enneus," said Sosylus. "I would advise you to tell them you are Campanian. Hannibal may well release any Campanians without ransom."

"I'm a Roman," replied Enneus. "Lying is for Carthaginians."

That remark abruptly ended any hope of Sosylus rendering assistance to the brat. I had sufficient authority to order young Enneus to be beaten or flogged, but I just said, "Enough of your insolence! If you talk this way to the man who will be your master, he will have you flogged!" I derived more satisfaction just from seeing the expression on the brat's face than from any beating or flogging I might have inflicted. Sosylus politely excused himself and I left young Enneus Tullius to his misery.

Hannibal did release all non-Roman captives without ransom. He told the allied captives: "I come not to place a yoke on Italy but to free her from the yoke of Rome."[3] He instructed them to go to their respective cities and towns and persuade their countrymen to make alliances with us. It was part of Hannibal's grand strategy to alienate as many of the native Italians as possible from Rome.

---

[3]    The Histories by Polybius Book 3, Page 85

## SANSARA, 217 B.C., LATE SUMMER

Hasdrubal received another dispatch from Italia, and he told Imilce that Hannibal had won another big victory over the Romans. I hoped this meant that the war would soon be over and Gisco would come home.

Imilce finally persuaded Hasdrubal to let her, Enidia, and me go on our expedition to visit our families. What he didn't know was that Enidia would not be coming back. Imilce and I would be in trouble when we got back, but it would be worth it.

We traveled by wagon to my village first. I brought both children and their nursemaid. I also brought Gisco's slave Motigon along to help carry baggage. He is Carpetani and the Carpetani speak a language similar to ours, so we communicate well. He is very loyal to Gisco and serves him without question. This is another thing about the Carthaginians that I don't understand. We had no slaves in my village. Of course women were expected to obey men, and younger people were expected to obey their elders, but no one owned anyone else. I asked Imilce what would happen to a slave if he refused to obey his master. She said that he would be whipped. Then I asked what would happen if he ran away. She said professional slave hunters would probably catch him and return him to the home of his master. He would then be whipped and made to wear chains.

We were accompanied by an escort of twenty soldiers and brought provisions to last for three months. It took two weeks to get to my village, and when we got near, I sent Motigon ahead to inform my relatives of our coming. A party of some thirty people is a big imposition on a small village like ours. I brought gifts for all my friends and relatives, expensive clothes and jewelry, which I hoped would smooth over any resentments about the inconvenience of having unexpected guests.

Everyone in the village seemed delighted to see us. They doted on the children and were gracious hosts to Imilce and Enidia. The escort and servants set up a camp on the outskirts of the village, but Mama and Manolo let me, my friends, and the children stay in their lodge. Manolo organized a hunting party and the men from the village brought back boar, deer, and rabbits so we could have a feast. There was enough to feed the whole village and our escort. The meal was a far cry from the rich fare we were used to eating in Khart Hadasht, but neither Imilce nor Enidia complained.

Grandfather summoned me to his lodge. He had aged and his hair was now entirely white. "How long do you plan to stay here, Sansara?" he asked me.

"For a week, with your permission, Grandfather," I replied.

"I am glad to see the children, Sansara," he said. "I am very proud of you. But why did your husband not come with you?"

"Gisco went to Italia with Hannibal to fight the Romans," I said. "We have received word that Hannibal has won two big victories already. I hope the war will end soon and Gisco can come back."

"Ah, the Romans," mused Grandfather. "A delegation of them came through our village just after the destruction of Saguntum to try to persuade me to support their cause. I said to them 'what kind of allies would you Romans be to the Volciani if you wouldn't even defend the Saguntines who have been your allies for so many years?' This Hannibal destroyed Saguntum and Arbocola, and it sounds as though he is wreaking destruction in Italia. I think it is better to have him for an ally than an enemy."

I laughed. "You're right, Grandfather. Hannibal is the last person you would want for an enemy."

"So you are happy and comfortable in Khart Hadasht?" asked Grandfather.

"I am lonely with Gisco gone, but the children keep me busy," I said. "It is very different from living here. I am trying to learn the Phoenician tongue so I can make friends and not feel so isolated. Imilce and Enidia have been very kind to me, but Enidia is going back to her own people. I will stay in Khart Hadasht and wait for Gisco to come back."

"You have done well, my child," said Grandfather, "and the Volciani benefit from the peace we have established with the Carthaginians. You can see that we have prospered from the cessation of warfare among the tribes."

"Yes, Grandfather," I said. "I just hope that the peace continues."

After spending a week in my village, we traveled eastward to the lands of the Turditani, and we delivered Enidia to her relatives there. She had never been happy in Khart Hadasht and she convinced her kinfolk that her marriage to Mago was a sham. She told them they had had a big quarrel before he left and that he had informed her that he intended to take a Carthaginian wife. Her mother was sympathetic and took her back into the household.

Castulo, where Imilce was born, is very different from Khart Hadasht. It is perhaps the biggest walled town in Spain that wasn't founded by either Greeks or Phoenicians. Its proximity to the silver mines has caused its population to swell. Imilce's father was the most important man in the city, and he lived in a large house, but it was nothing compared to the palace we lived in in Khart Hadasht. Castulo seemed to me to be halfway between my village and Khart Hadasht in its standard of living and degree of civilization. Clearly it had been less jarring for Imilce to make the transition to Carthaginian civilization than it had been for me or Enidia to do so. Imilce's parents welcomed us and we stayed for two weeks under their roof.

Hasdrubal met us when we returned to Khart Hadasht. "Where's Enidia?" he asked.

"She decided to stay with her parents," said Imilce.

"And you let her?" asked Hasdrubal with an angry scowl. "What will Mago say when he gets back?"

"You know your brother cares not for Enidia, nor she for him," said Imilce. "The Turditani are loyal allies of Carthage because

Hannibal defended them against the Saguntines. Mago's marriage to Enidia is not necessary to secure their loyalty. Mago wants a Carthaginian wife and Enidia wants to be free of Mago. This way they both get what they want."

"I should have the two of you whipped," grumbled Hasdrubal. "And I would if you were not Hannibal's wife, and Sansara the mother to Gisco's babies."

We made a show of being contrite, but when we were alone together we hugged each other and dissolved into giggles.

# FIVE

## FABIAN TACTICS



I wonder if the Romans are getting smart," said Mago. "Their new leader, Quintus Fabius Maximus, is avoiding an engagement. He interferes with our foraging and lays waste to the land before we can plunder it, but he won't confront us in a pitched battle! I think he plans to starve us out."

We were barely getting by on what little we had to eat, so I replied, "That sounds like a good strategy. He may just succeed."

"Hannibal won't permit that," said Mago emphatically. "We're heading toward Casinum to meet with the Capuans. If we can make an alliance with them, they'll provide us with all we need. It's a rich territory."

Unfortunately, when Hannibal told the native guides that he wanted them to take us to Casinum, they misunderstood him and proceeded to take us to Casilinum, which was in the wrong direction. When Hannibal learned of the mistake, he was furious. He had the two guides scourged and crucified; but the damage was done.

Fabius had us in a difficult position. The territory around Casilinum grew mostly grapes, and you can't feed an army on grapes. We had to get to a more productive region, but the only way out was through a defile where Fabius could trap us and slaughter our forces. Hannibal, however, came up with an ingenious solution. We had acquired a herd of 2,000 oxen by plunder. He had us attach bundles of kindling to the horns of the oxen, and, when night came, we set the kindling on fire and drove the beasts through the defile. The animals went mad with pain; their bellowing filled the night air. The Romans guarding the pass panicked and ran off, and we were able to march unmolested through the pass and back into Apulia. I'm surprised that old Fabius didn't die from apoplexy right then and there!

Unfortunately for Fabius, the Roman people weren't impressed with his strategy. His Master of Horse, Marcus Rufus Minucius, was elevated to become his equal in command. Fabius and Minucius had divided up their forces and had separated their camps. Hannibal quickly took the measure of Minucius. He was a fool like Sempronius and Flaminius had been.

"Mago," said Hannibal. "I think we have another chance for an ambush! My scouts tell me that Minucius and Fabius have separated their camps, and my spies tell me that Minucius is spoiling for a pitched battle. There's a hill nearby that would be of benefit to whichever side can occupy it. At its base is an expanse of land that is perfect for hiding thousands of soldiers. We'll station a small number of men to visibly occupy the summit and you take five thousand men to hide in the crevasses at the base."

Minucius snapped at the bait, and when he and his legionaries tried to capture the strategic hill, Mago's men emerged from their hiding places.

Hannibal asked me to stay with him while he observed the battle, because he knew that I had keen eyesight. I could see the fighting going on below us. Minucius and his men had been completely surprised, and it was not going well for the Romans. Then suddenly I saw a cloud of dust in the distance. "Hannibal!" I cried, "there's a huge force of Romans riding this way to relieve Minucius!"

"By all the gods!" exclaimed Hannibal. "That rascal Fabius! I never expected him to stir! Call the retreat!"

Minucius and most of his men were miraculously saved, and Minucius had little choice other than to kiss Fabius's posterior. That night in camp Hannibal said, "Verily, did I not often prophesy that the cloud we saw hovering above the heights would one day burst upon us in a drenching and furious storm?"[4]

Hannibal knew what a contentious lot the Romans were, so he devised a strategy to undermine Fabius politically. He sent Maharbal and the Numidian cavalry up to Etruria and told them to lay waste to all the territory up there, but spare Fabius's estate. This certainly caused grumbling among the Romans. The old fox managed to manipulate his way out of this snare as well. We had negotiated a prisoner exchange, but there were more prisoners on their side than ours, so the Romans owed us a pound and one-half of silver for each of the excess two hundred and forty-seven men. The Roman Senate declined to provide the money, so Fabius sold his estate in Etruria to personally pay the debt. This, no doubt, had the effect of silencing his critics for a time.

But Fabius's critics didn't stay quiet for long. His dictatorship expired after six months and was not renewed. The consulship reverted to Cneius Servilius Geminus, and Marcus Atilius Regulus, who replaced the fallen Flaminius. These two Consuls followed Fabius's policy of not engaging us in pitched battle, but the Romans grew impatient and elected a Consul whose sworn intention was

---

[4]    Life of Quintus Fabius Maximus by Plutarch, paragraph 19

to end this war once and for all. His name was Gaius Terentius Varro, and he boasted that he would bring the war to a conclusion the very day he got sight of the enemy. The Greeks have a word for this: *hubris*.

# SIX

## THE BATTLE OF CANNAE

GISCO
216 B.C.

We spent the summer in Apulia living off the land. Unfortunately, the land was soon depleted, and it was clearly evident that we could not maintain ourselves much longer unless we moved on and made some conquests in the south. Hannibal had thus far not persuaded any of the Italian or Greek inhabitants of Italia to come over to our side. The Gauls were of help militarily, but could not keep us fed. Then, in August of that year, the gods answered our prayers. The Romans, under their new Consuls Gaius Terentius Varro and Lucius Aemilius Paullus, raised a huge army and came out to Apulia to annihilate us.

Our camp was on a hill, and we watched as the Romans mobilized their troops. It was a huge mass, and I must have looked awestricken because Hannibal came up to me and asked me what I was thinking.

"They must have twice as many men as we do, Commander!" I replied.

Hannibal grinned. "But there is one thing that has escaped your notice, Gisco," he said.

"What's that?" I asked.

"You see all of those men out there?" he said. "Among all of those men, there is not a single one named Gisco!"[5]

Mago, Maharbal, Carthalo, Solylus, Hanno, and Bomilcar all began to laugh. Word of Hannibal's jest spread and soon everyone was laughing. I hoped we'd still be laughing at the end of this day!

We were on the north side of the Aufidus River, with our backs to the river. The Romans lined up north of us, facing the river. They lined up in their usual assemblage with the *hastati*, the less experienced troops, in front, the *principes*, more experienced troops, behind them, and the *triarii*, the veterans, in the rear. Hannibal expected them to try to break through our lines, which is exactly what he wanted them to do, because his strategy was one of envelopment. He placed the Gallic and Spanish troops in the center, and the African troops on the flanks. Our Numidian cavalry was on our right flank and our Spanish and Gallic cavalry was on the left. Our front line appeared to be in a convex formation. The Roman hastati advanced into our front line and started to push the Gauls and Spanish troops back, so that the front line soon became concave. Hannibal instructed the troops in the van to retreat slowly. He sent the African troops on the flanks forward, and with time the whole of the Roman infantry was enveloped. In the meantime, our cavalry on both flanks dealt with the Roman cavalry, driving them from the field. On the left flank the Roman Consul, Lucius Aemilius Paulus, was hit in the head with a rock launched by one of our Balearic slingers. Although he was wearing a helmet he must

---

[5]    Ibid. Paragraph 22

have sustained a concussion because he dismounted from his horse, and, much to Hannibal's joy, most of his horsemen did the same. Hannibal commented, "This is better than if they had all been delivered to me in chains!"[6]

Once the Roman infantry were surrounded, we crowded in on them so that they had no room to maneuver. All that remained was to cut them all down. To me there was little satisfaction in it. If I'm going to kill, I prefer a contest, and this was like spearing rats in a barrel. It was a chore, and we were all exhausted by the end of the day. Not that I would complain about the outcome of the battle. Cannae would take its place alongside the battle of Marathon and the battle of Gaugamela as one of the most one-sided victories in the history of warfare. We believed that we were well on the way to becoming masters of the civilized world. We had destroyed nearly three-fourths of the Roman forces. We could not imagine that there was any way the Romans would ever recover their military strength. The Romans who survived the battle gathered at Canusium, a town south of the Aufidus River. We were too exhausted to pursue them. We did capture some ten thousand men in the two Roman camps.

The day after the battle, Hannibal gave the order to go among the dead on the battlefield and collect the gold signet rings from those who belonged to the wealthier classes. It was a gruesome task. The battlefield was covered with tens of thousands of dead Romans and we had to work quickly because the stench, already powerful, would soon become intolerable. Above us multitudes of carrion-eating birds circled indolently, occasionally coming down to peck at a dead soldier's eye. The only sounds were the birds' raucous cries, the buzzing of flies attracted by filth, and the occasional moans of the wounded. As I walked among the dead my eyes met those of a live, but badly wounded, Roman. He looked to be about my age, and his scant growth of beard indicated that he followed

---

[6]    Ibid. Paragraph 23

the custom of upper class Roman men of shaving their beards. He beckoned to me with his hand. He moved his breastplate to expose his heart and pointed to it. I nodded. He shut his eyes tightly and I plunged my sword into his heart. This was exactly what I would want if I were in this Roman's situation; a quick death with only the briefest of pain. I had been taught that death on the battlefield in defense of one's country is the most noble of ends. If any Romans are left alive after we finish with this war, the deceased soldier will be much honored by his family. I took the gold signet ring from his finger and also took his dagger, a well-made Roman *pugio*. A moment of compassion possessed me and I took a bronze coin from my pack and placed it in his mouth. This would purchase his passage across the river Styx into Hades.

We had lost close to six thousand men on our side. We collected their bodies and built a pyre to burn them. Most of the dead were Gallic tribesmen, and their fellows performed their native rituals to speed their souls to the afterlife. We did not have the resources to dispose of the Roman dead, and the Romans were not around to see to it, so some fifty thousand Roman bodies were left to rot on the field where they fell.

In one instance we found a Numidian alive underneath a pile of dead Romans. His face was mutilated from being bitten by a furious dying Roman soldier.

We found the battered body of the Roman Consul Lucius Aemilius Paullus, readily identifiable by his red cloak and signet ring. Hannibal treated the body with all due respect, building a pyre and holding a funeral for him the next day. Hannibal himself delivered encomiums in praise of the Consul's courage and his devotion to his nation. This respectful treatment of a fallen enemy stood in great contrast to the way the Romans treated fallen Carthaginian generals during this war.

We gathered over two hundred rings, and Hannibal had them put into an urn. Maharbal was eager to follow up our victory with the conquest of the city of Rome itself. "Let me take the cavalry to Rome and you can meet me there in five days," he told Hannibal.

Hannibal, however, was not eager to lay siege to Rome. "We have no siege equipment, Maharbal, and we have no provisions to sustain ourselves during a long siege."

Exasperated, Maharbal exclaimed, "It seems the gods don't grant all their gifts to one man," he said. "You know very well how to win a victory, Hannibal, but you don't know how to use one."[7]

"I'm sending Carthalo to Rome along with ten well-born Roman prisoners. The prisoners will plead to be ransomed, and Carthalo will deliver our peace terms."

"What sort of peace terms are you proposing?" asked Maharbal.

"Essentially the same terms that Rome imposed upon Carthage after the last war. They will have to return to us all the islands in the western Mediterranean that they took from us, as well as those parts of Sicily that we once occupied. They will have to confine their military activities to the Italian peninsula and they will have to pay us a heavy indemnity in gold and silver."

If Hannibal thought that the Romans would be reasonable in the face of this monumental defeat, he was deluded. The Romans allowed a spokesman for the prisoners to present their case before the Senate, then proceeded to reject any notion of ransoming prisoners and even forbade private citizens from ransoming their kin. They would not even permit Carthalo to enter the city to deliver peace terms. Once again our prisoners would have to be sold to Greek slave traders, as they couldn't be used for ransom.

Nevertheless, we soon began to experience the benefits of our great victory. One by one the cities of southern Italia outside the region of Latium allied themselves with us. Most important was the city of Capua in Campania. The Atellani, the Calatini, the Hirpini, some of the Apulians, most of the Samnites, the Lucanians and the Surrentinians came over to our side. In Magna Graecia, the

---

[7]    Ab Urbe Condita by Titus Livius, Book XXII.51

area of southern Italia that had been settled by Greeks, the cities of Metapontum, Croton, Locri, and, eventually, Tarentum, allied with us. Only Nola and Neapolis stubbornly clung to the Romans.

# SEVEN

## MAGO AND GISCO
## RETURN TO CARTHAGE

GISCO
215 B.C.

Hannibal divided our army. He brought most of the troops to Capua to cement his alliance with that city. They would winter there, and, for a few months, enjoy a life of feasting, drinking, and the pleasures of the company of women. Mago, however, was sent into Lucania and Bruttium to gather up our allies there and to subdue any resistance, and I went with him. Mago gave thought to attempting to conquer Neapolis, but was deterred by the strength of its walls. Mago had brought along the urn that contained all of the gold signet rings we had collected from the highborn Roman dead after Cannae. These rings would make an impressive spectacle when he returned to Carthage.

"Gisco," he said. "Why don't you come with me to Carthage? Hannibal needs money, reinforcements, and supplies, and I plan to take our case to the Senate."

I leapt at the chance to see my family again after over two year's absence. I also admit that I had had my fill of war. There are those who delight in it, but I was not one of them. We sailed to Carthage from Bruttium. When we arrived we were hailed as conquering heroes. Every night we were wined and dined and persuaded to tell of our experiences and conquests. I had never felt so honored and important. At these parties Mago would work the crowd and try to drum up support for the war effort. He was ably assisted by members of the Barca faction, particularly Himilco, and my brother Hasdrubal. My brother was rapidly becoming more and more influential in Carthaginian politics.

We were granted an audience by the Senate. It was Mago's moment to shine. He took Hannibal's urn with all of the gold signet rings and poured it out on the floor of the Senate. "These rings are a token of our great victory over Rome at Cannae." He said. "Only Romans of the two upper classes, the nobility and the *equites*, wear these rings. For every Roman nobleman or *eques* we found dead on the field of Cannae, two hundred or so lesser souls also perished.

"In the past two years since we entered Italia, we have won four victories on the battlefield—at the river Ticinus, at the river Trebia, at Lake Trasimene, and at Cannae. We have slain over one hundred thousand of the enemy, we have slain two sitting Consuls and at least three former Consuls. We have made alliances with many of the Gauls of northern Italia, and now, after the battle of Cannae, we have made alliances with most of the peoples of Campania, Apulia, Samnium, Lucania, and Magna Graecia. We are poised to end Rome's dominance over Italia and over the western Mediterranean.

"But these victories have come at a cost," Mago continued, "after four battles our ranks are thinned; and we cannot count on the Gauls to stay with us permanently. Many of them have gone home to their families. Our elephants did not survive the cold first winter in the north, so we will need more. We need food and wine, and we need money to win the cooperation of the natives that we have succeeded in alienating from Rome. And most of all we need reinforcements to bring our troop level up to strength. We are asking the great city of Carthage to support us. Carthage has much to gain from our victory in this war. This is no time to slacken our effort!"

Shouts of jubilation filled the Senate house and nearly everyone cheered Mago's words loud and long. Only old Hanno the Great sat silent and unsmiling. Finally, when the cheering died down, Himilco turned to face Hanno and shouted "What now, Hanno? Do you still regret that we chose Hannibal as our military leader? Do you still regret that we started this war?"

Hanno rose. "I would have preferred to remain silent upon this occasion and not seek to spoil your joy at these tidings Mago brings, but since Himilco calls upon me to answer, it would be rude and haughty of me not to make my opinion known. Yes, I still regret that we made Hannibal our military leader, and yes, I still do regret that we have started this war. You are asking for money, supplies, and reinforcements, the same things you would be asking for if you had been defeated, rather than victorious. Let me ask a question of you, Mago. You say that many of the peoples of Italia have revolted against Rome. Tell me, have any of the thirty-five tribes of Latium deserted the Roman cause?"

"No." replied Mago.

"That means that Rome still has considerable reserves of loyal allies to draw upon for its armies. One other question: Has Rome sent any emissaries to sue for peace?"

"No." replied Mago.

"Then we are still at war, the same as we were when Hannibal's army first entered Italia. These victories change nothing. How often victory shifted in the previous war, as many of us are alive to remember. Never did our fortunes seem more favorable on land and sea than they did before the consulships of Gaius Lutatius and Aulus Postumius, but in the consulships of Lutatius and Postumius we were utterly defeated off the Aegates islands.

"The fortunes of war can change drastically, and I say that now is the best time to restore peace, when we are at the height of victory and can make a peace favorable to ourselves. I say that rather than send more supplies, gold, and mercenaries to Hannibal, we put a stop to this war now. Otherwise we will regret it someday, when the Romans get the upper hand."[8]

Few in the Senate paid any heed to the counsel of old Hanno, and it was decided to send reinforcements to Hannibal.

Mago and I had been so lean when we returned from Italia that we almost resembled ill-treated slaves. I felt blessed by Ba-al to be back with my family and eating like a king every night. Aba, Uma, Buba, my brother Hasdrubal, his wife and children and usually several guests would sit around and listen to my stories of the war in Italia. We were all strong Barca supporters; everyone, that is, except Buba. Perhaps it was the mental deterioration that comes with old age; she had no inhibitions about speaking her mind, no matter how many of us disagreed with her.

"Old Hanno is right!" she would say. "We should end this war now! I pray to Tanit that I don't live to see my grandsons end up like my Gisco!"

Drubal joked. "Your grandsons don't get crucified, Buba. They crucify." In my brother's case this would prove to be no joke.

---

[8]    Ibid Book XXIII.12,13

# EIGHT

## BACK TO SPAIN

GISCO
215 B.C.

I was not looking forward to going back to Italia, as I had few fond memories of the place. Melqart answered my prayers, although not in the manner I would have desired. Hasdrubal Barca, the brother of Hannibal, had just suffered a major defeat at the hands of the Roman generals Publius and Cneius Scipio in a place called Dertosa. He had lost most of his infantry, and our entire enterprise in Spain was now in jeopardy. The Senate decided that both Mago and my brother Drubal would bring armies to Spain to reinforce Hasdrubal Barca. Hannibal would receive only 4,000 Numidians and 20 elephants. The long-range plan was that once we defeated the Scipios in Spain, Hasdrubal Barca himself would travel over the Alps with his army and join up with Hannibal. I was happy to be going back to Spain as Mago's lieutenant. I looked forward to seeing Sansara and my daughter Giscana. I hoped that Sansara had not taken up with another man in my absence, but there was no way to know.

I assisted Mago in recruiting Numidian horsemen, Balearic slingers, and Liby-Phoenician infantry from the kingdom of Syphax. The Numidians were led by Masinissa, the son of King Gala of the Massylii. He was a tall, lean, and handsome devil with a mane of curly black hair. He was the best horseman you'd ever hope to see, so much at one with his horse that you might have taken him for a centaur. He attracted attention everywhere he went, and the women swooned over him. Even little girls, such as my seven-year-old niece, Caphonbal, couldn't take their eyes off of him.

When all was ready we took transports to Khart Hadasht. My brother Drubal brought along his wife Amashtar and their children Bomilcar and Caphonbal. He lodged them in the palace. I went to my old quarters at the palace hoping to find Sansara, but half expecting her to be gone. Much to my surprise and delight she was still there. She had filled out during the past two years and looked more appealing than ever. When she saw me she squealed and ran up to me, throwing her arms around me, "My Gisco! I didn't think you come back!" I smiled at her. "I so happy now!" she proclaimed.

"You've learned a lot of Phoenician, Sansara. Who taught you?"

"My Giscana," she replied. "She insist I speak Phoenician." She turned toward the opening to the other room. "Giscana!" she shouted. "Come see you Aba! Bring little Gisco!" Two young children came through the door, along with their nurse. I recognized Giscana, who was now five years old, but there was also a two-year-old boy that I had never seen. Sansara picked up the little boy and presented him to me. "Gisco, this is you Aba!" The child wriggled and started to cry.

"Sansara," I said. "This is my son?"

"Yes," she replied. "I not know I pregnant when you leave. Must have been from our last night." I was overwhelmed. This was good fortune beyond my wildest hopes. Now I had a wife who could speak to me and I had just found out that I was father to a son!

I sensed that little Gisco was not ready for the stranger who was his father. I would have to be patient. Giscana was more receptive and I took her in my arms and asked all the questions you might ask of a five-year-old.

"How old are you?" I asked her.

"Five and a half," she replied.

"Can you read?"

"No, but I know the *alif bet* and I can count to 20," she said.

"I'm going to teach you how to read," I said.

She spoke perfect Phoenician without any Spanish accent. She was pretty, like her mother. Sansara led me to a couch and served me flatbread, wine, and fruit. She sat beside me and stroked my hair and beard. "We sleep together tonight, but first you take bath." She laughed.

"For you I'll jump into the sea." I replied.

I excused myself after a few hours, telling Sansara that I had to see Mago, but that I would be back. Mago was in his quarters in the palace. His Turditani bride had returned to her own people, but he did not seem particularly upset about it. He had never gotten her pregnant. When I told him about my little Gisco, he grinned and offered me his congratulations. "This calls for some good wine!" he said, and brought out an amphora of Falernian wine that he had managed to bring from Italia.

"What are our plans now?" I asked.

"We are recruiting in northern Spain," he said. "We have signed on Indibilis and his brother Mandonius, the chieftains of the Ilergites. We are also trying to keep the Celtiberians from assisting the Romans. They're an unstable lot, and difficult to deal with. I don't really think that we can rely on them as allies, but there may be advantages in keeping them neutral. Our first priority is to hold onto all of the Carthaginian sphere of influence south of the Iberus, and then we want to clear a corridor so that my brother Hasdrubal can lead an army over the Pyrenees and then into Italia."

"I'm not doing that one again!" I proclaimed. Mago laughed.

"There is plenty for you to do right here in Spain," he said. "We suspect that at some point the Scipios are going to go on the offensive and we want to be ready for them."

There was well-appointed bathhouse in the palace. I had the slaves heat up a hot bath and I soaked in it until the water became tepid. Then I had them massage my back and anoint my body with fragrant oils.

Finally, I was ready to do my duty as a husband, a task I had been forced to neglect for more than two years. There is nothing like the act of love when you haven't done it in a while! We were both more than ready and we went at it like a lion and a lioness! She was just insatiable. I was so exhausted by morning that I slept most of the next day. I had no idea how this night would alter the course of my life.

After our spectacular beginning in Italia, Hannibal seemed to lose momentum. The Romans had no intention of giving in or making peace. Hannibal's intention was to capture a seaport on the Mediterranean Sea, in order to have unimpeded access to supplies and reinforcements from Carthage, but the Romans fought hard to prevent this. Having learned their lesson from Cannae, the Romans no longer sought pitched battles but carried on a dogged war of attrition, gradually capturing back territories that had defected to Hannibal in the aftermath of Cannae.

Here in Spain our situation became more and more difficult. In the aftermath of the battle of Dertosa, more and more of our allies were defecting to the Romans. These included the towns of Iliturgis and Castulo, both uncomfortably close to where we had the huge silver mines that contributed so much to the prosperity of Carthage. Mago and Hasdrubal Barca made it their priority to retake these two cities, and we lay siege to Iliturgis, where there was a Roman garrison. This drew Gneius Scipio, who attacked us with a legion of troops and raised the siege. We lost over 12,000 slain and 1,000 taken prisoner. We then attempted to lay siege to Bigerra, which had also defected to the Romans, but Gneius Scipio drove us off. We withdrew our camp to Munda, but Scipio followed, and we engaged in a pitched battle. We were losing badly, but the Romans withdrew after their Proconsul was wounded in the thigh. We lost 15,000 slain or captured in this battle. We withdrew to Aurinx. Scipio followed once again and engaged our forces, slaying or capturing another 9,000, mostly Gallic mercenaries recently recruited by Mago. Then the Romans took back the site of the city of Saguntum, where the war had begun, and re-established the city, having gathered up the few survivors of the siege. It had been a disastrous year for Carthage in Spain.

## SANSARA
## 215 B.C.

Gisco has come home to me at last! He was impressed with my ability to speak Phoenician and he adores his son. The night he came home we made love all night long. I just couldn't get enough of him. I had been waiting for so long! Now I'm sure I'm with child again; my milk has dried up and I've had to wean little Gisco.

Unfortunately, the war continues, and Gisco has gone off again with Mago. Since Hasdrubal lost that big battle at Dertosa the Romans have made inroads into southern Spain. Imilce is distressed that her beloved Castulo has gone over to the Romans. I hope that my people, the Volciani, can avoid being drawn into this war. Last year we learned that Hannibal had won a huge victory over the Romans in Italia; yet the Romans fight on, they will not surrender or make peace. So much death, so much destruction. What has Hannibal wrought? I only wish that all of this would end, that I could have my Gisco to myself, and we could raise our children in peace.

Gisco's brother Drubal has also brought an army to Spain. He has brought his wife and children to Khart Hadasht and now they occupy an apartment in the palace. Gisco and Drubal don't get along. They are civil on the surface, but I can tell that they don't like each other. I have tried to be friendly to Drubal's wife Amashtar and to their two children, Caphonbal and Bomilcar, but she seems to have the attitude that some Carthaginians have, that we Spaniards are beneath them. Caphonbal is very pretty and very spoiled, and she lords it over Giscana.

# NINE

## THE EVIL EYE

GISCO
214 B.C.

In winter I returned to Khart Hadasht to find Sansara big with child. Within a month she had our second son, whom we named Hanno. Our little Hanno was a most beautiful baby, with fair skin like his mother's, gray eyes, and chestnut hair. He attracted attention wherever we went. We took him to the temple of Tanit and Ba-al Hammon to ask their blessing, and also to the temple of Eshmoun to petition the god to grant the child health. In each instance we sacrificed a lamb, as is the custom. The child's spectacular beauty made me uneasy, because it is well known that beautiful children attract the evil eye.

When spring arrived, Mago led our forces to the Upper Baetis, where we took up positions to protect our silver mines. We could not let these mines fall into the hands of the Romans. A few days before the summer solstice, I received a messenger from Khart Hadasht who brought me a summons from the high priest of the temple of Tanit and Ba-al Hammon. The messenger made obeisance to me and said "Rab Gisco, my master, Indibal, high priest of Ba-al Hammon and his consort Tanit, wishes you to attend an audience with him. It concerns a matter of utmost importance." Utterly perplexed, I brought the summons to Mago. He was as perplexed as I was.

"You did make the proper sacrifices when your last son was born, didn't you?" he laughed.

"Of course!" I said. "Who would be foolish enough to deny the gods their sacrifices?"

Mago sighed. "I suppose you had better go and see what this is all about," he said. "While you are there you can arrange for a transport of wine, and also supplies for our new recruits. They'll need sandals, tunics, swords, spears, and shields. My brother Hasdrubal is sending us 500 newly recruited Ilergites and I'm expecting them to arrive in about a week."

It was two days' ride on horseback to Khart Hadasht. I brought along my two body slaves Palonis and Motigon.

I arrived to find my wife in distress. She had heard snatches of conversation here and there, which she couldn't quite comprehend but had found disturbing. Women had been looking furtively at little Hanno and then turning away, apparently fighting tears. "Why are you home so soon, my husband?" she asked. "I don't understand what is happening. All of these women who used to be so nice and friendly to me, they avoid me. What have I done?"

I had no answer for her. "I don't know what's going on, Sansara, but I will find out. I suspect it may have something to do with Ba-al."

"I don't understand," said Sansara. "Have I offended Ba-al? I didn't intend to. I don't understand your Carthaginian gods. We have our own gods among my people."

"I'm sure you have done nothing to offend Ba-al. I will talk to the priest and find out what is going on." I took her in my arms, kissed her lips, and stroked her hair. "Let us relax tonight and feast and make love. I will talk to the priest tomorrow." I picked up each of the children in turn and hugged and kissed them. Giscana was now six, Gisco three and Hanno five months. When I went to pick him up, Hanno held out his arms and smiled with pleasure. He trusted me completely.

The next day I climbed up to the Byrsa and entered the temple of Tanit. I was ushered in to see Indibal, the *Rab Kohanim*, or high priest. Indibal sat on a golden throne. He was dressed in a long robe, richly embroidered with images of birds, animals, sacred plants, and heavenly bodies. He was a short man, but his striking and elaborate headdress rendered him imposing. The smell of incense hung heavily in the stagnant air. Behind him I could see a larger-than-life statue of the goddess Tanit, a serene smile on her face, like that of a mother contemplating her sleeping children. "You sent for me, Holy One?" I asked.

"Yes, Gisco, son of Gisco. Welcome. You are blessed of Tanit and of Ba-al Hammon." He replied in a high-pitched, nasal voice. "You are the one by whose sacrifice Carthage will be saved."

"Sacrifice? I don't understand." This did not sound good.

"You must have perceived how the gods have turned away from Carthage in the past year. It has been divined that Tanit and Ba-al Hammon demand sacrifice, and that this must be a perfect male child. We have made a search and you are the only one who possesses a child of this quality. I know that this is not an easy thing for you to do, but your nation demands this sacrifice of you, and it must be carried out."

I was stunned. "No. I can't permit this. My wife is not Carthaginian, she won't understand. It would kill her."

"Your wife, Sansara, is blessed among women," said Indibal. "Tanit will favor her with whatever she desires."

"No!" I said, "I can't…I can't."

"Gisco, son of Gisco, refusing the gods is not an option. Our entire nation is at stake. Bring the child here at dawn tomorrow morning. You may go."

# TEN

## GISCO THE TRAITOR

GISCO
214 B.C.

I made the customary obeisance and left. I had to think. Refusing the gods is not an option, Indibal had said. But I knew that refusing the gods was my only option. I had never thought much about the cult of Tanit and Ba-al Hammon. I knew that child sacrifice took place but had believed it to be a voluntary matter. You offered the life of your child as a gift of gratitude if, for example, you recovered from a painful illness. I never realized that it could be forced upon you. Indibal seemed to have every confidence that I would comply. Evidently the sacrifice had to appear to be voluntary on the part of the parents. I was now in a position where I had to choose between two unthinkable options, to sacrifice my son as a burnt offering, or to become a traitor to my country. I knew that the only place my son would be safe would be the part of Spain securely occupied by Rome, and the only way we could live there in safety would be for me to sell myself to the Romans. Even that course would be risky. The Romans might not accept my offer. They might crucify me and sell Sansara and the children into slavery, but I felt even that was a better prospect than what I now faced.

I went to my quarters in the palace and summoned my two slaves. When Palonis and Motigon arrived I said: "You have both served me well and I require only one more day of service from you, and then you will be free to return to your own homes. I am leaving Khart Hadasht to go north and I ask only that you help me get away from here. Then you will be free."

Palonis and Motigon stared at each other in amazement. Palonis was of mixed Greek and Spanish extraction and Motigon was Carpetani. They were both short and stocky men in their thirties, with bushy hair and beards. Both had been captured as prepubescent boys. They had been in the service of my family for many years and were as close as brothers. "We are pleased that you are granting us our freedom, but we do not wish to leave you. You have been a good master," said Palonis.

"It is dangerous where I am going," I replied. "If we are captured either by the Carthaginians or the Romans you could be crucified, or, at best, enslaved to a worse master."

"We prefer to take our chances, Master," said Motigon. "You will be much safer if we accompany you. You must think of your lady and your little children. When you have reached safety we will avail ourselves of our freedom."

I smiled. "I am most grateful to you both. I will pay you for your services, and you are free to leave whenever you wish. What I need you to do is to bring four horses here from the stable, one for each of you and one each for me and my wife. We will leave after nightfall. We have little time to prepare."

I went to my wife's chamber. "Sansara, we must leave tonight and bring the children. We will travel on horseback. Quickly pack clothes for yourself and the children, and any food that can be safely stored. Just bring what's necessary, we must travel lightly."

"What is it, Gisco? What has happened?"

I didn't want to upset her too much, but she needed to realize the urgency of the situation. "It's little Hanno. They want him for a sacrifice. I won't let it happen. We must leave as soon as night falls."

She hugged me and began to cry. "Why? Why Hanno? He's just a baby!"

"They think the sacrifice will help Carthage, but I don't care. It's not something I can do."

"I love you, Gisco," she said. "You're right, we must go. Shall we go back to my people, the Volciani?"

"Are the Volciani still with Carthage or have they gone over to the Romans?" I asked.

"I don't know," she replied.

"I think that either way it would be dangerous." I said. "I think I must deal with the Romans directly."

"Deal with the Romans? But..."

"Yes I know. Treason," I said, "but the Romans don't practice child sacrifice."

"Very well," she said. "There is a lot to do to get ready."

I gathered up all the gold coins I could find and stashed them in various places. I found out who would be guarding the gate from which we would leave, and bribed them to take no notice of us. I also stopped by the military supply depot and arranged for the supplies Mago had requested.

I wished that I could have said good-bye to Mago and explained the reason for my defection. We had been friends since we were four or five. Some of my earliest memories were of following him around. We had lived in the part of Carthage called Megara. It was where wealthier citizens dwelt, and was full of streams and gardens. In summer the two of us would wander about and gorge ourselves on ripe fruit. I was always in awe of Mago, who, although only a few months older than I, was far more confident and outgoing. We had never been separated for very long. I would miss him. Would he understand? I had no idea.

Palonis and Motigon returned and said that the horses were ready. "My wife will carry little Hanno in a sling," I said. "Each of you can carry one of the other children. If we are accosted by soldiers, either Carthaginian or Roman, just ride off with the child to safety. I will be armed and will keep the soldiers occupied."

"I can't believe you're doing this," said Motigon.

"What choice do I have?" I asked.

"Could you not go to Rab Mago and ask him to intervene?" he asked.

"I fear Indibal's men will get there first and alert the soldiers, so I won't even get to see Mago. I think it would be better to go in a direction where there will be no soldiers. Anyway, it's bad enough that I am risking bringing the wrath of the gods down on myself. I don't think it would be right to involve Mago. He's much more important to Carthage than I am and he needs the gods on his side."

We departed Khart Hadasht in darkness, and my bribes allowed us to leave unnoticed. Fortunately, the moon was mostly full. I was dressed in full armor and carried a shield as well as javelins and a *falcata*. We made progress slowly; Sansara was not very experienced at riding, and she had to nurse Hanno from time to time.

We did not stop to rest. We ate on horseback and continued to ride during the morning. I wanted to get as far from Khart Hadasht as possible. We took the path toward the northeast, which, I hoped, would lead to Tarraco. That afternoon, a delegation from Khart Hadasht caught up with us. There were five of them. I sent the others ahead and turned to face them, drawing my sword.

"Gisco, son of Gisco, where are you going?" I recognized the speaker. He was the priest who had escorted me to my interview with Indibal the morning before. I also recognized Memon, the executioner. These were not soldiers, at least not soldiers of my own quality. They had more to fear from me than I had from them.

"I am a free citizen and I do not have to tell you where I am going," I replied.

"You are a soldier of Carthage and subject to our rule," said the priest.

"My superior is Mago Barca, and I take my orders from him, not you," I said. "And you are right, I am a soldier. I killed hundreds of Romans at Trebia, Trasimene, and Cannae. I have never killed a Carthaginian and I would prefer not to do so now. To get to my son you will have to come through me. Take me if you think you can, but I guarantee that some of you will die."

"So you refuse to obey the wishes of Tanit and Ba-al Hammon," said the priest. "You will be cursed of the gods!"

"That is my problem, not yours," I said. "If you value your lives, turn around and go back to Khart Hadasht. Even if you take me, my freedmen are also armed."

The priest looked at Memon. Memon shook his head. "This man is beloved of Mago Barca. Let him go on his way. Surely there are other infants whose parents love Carthage more than they love themselves." I made no reply to that, but thought to myself, I don't love myself more than I love Carthage, I love my wife and children more than I love Carthage. Memon then addressed me, saying, "The next time I see you, Gisco, son of Gisco, it is likely that I will be driving spikes into your wrists and feet, nailing them to a cross. Farewell until then." With that, the party turned around and headed back toward Khart Hadasht.

## MAGO

It had been over a week since Gisco had gone to Khart Hadasht and he had still not returned. This was not like Gisco. Say what you will about his quirks, he is as reliable as sunrise. He is also the best man I have for training new recruits and for resolving disputes among the soldiers. I couldn't imagine why he was taking so long to come back.

"Memon, what are you doing here?" I asked the executioner when he rode into our camp with a priest of Ba-al Hammon and several other officials from Khart Hadasht.

"We have come to lodge a complaint against your lieutenant, Gisco, son of Gisco," replied Memon.

"What has he done?" I asked.

"He has taken his wife and children from Khart Hadasht without permission," said Memon, "and when he was last seen he was heading north toward territory held by Rome. He drew his sword against us and threatened to cut anyone down who tried to stop him. We had no choice but to let him go on his way."

I was truly puzzled. "But why would Gisco do that?" I asked.

The priest spoke. "Indibal, the Rab Kohanim of Ba-al Hammon and Tanit, had had a vision and divined that the God and Goddess are demanding a sacrifice, a perfect male child. Gisco's younger son was chosen. Gisco has chosen to defy the gods."

"What?" I cried. "This is madness! There will be no human sacrifices to the gods while the House of Barca rules in Spain! My brother Hasdrubal will agree with me, and so would Hannibal if he were here. You can tell Indibal that if I hear of any such observances, I will personally burn his temple down, with him inside of it! Now go back to Khart Hadasht, all of you. I will deal with Gisco."

They left. But what was I to do about Gisco? He might well be in Roman-held territory by now. If he were allowed to go through with his intentions he could do us a lot of harm. Even he is not so naïve as to believe that the Romans would grant him asylum without asking something in return, and he has a lot to offer them. He must be stopped. If we could find him before he contacts the Romans we could assure him that there will be no child sacrifice and persuade him to come back.

I'll send Mazeus after him, I thought. Gisco likes and trusts him. Once he contacts the Romans we will have no choice but to find him, bring him back, and crucify him as a traitor. This truly galls me. A pox on those cursed priests!

# ELEVEN

## THE ROMANS

Gisco
214 B.C.

I was happy that the encounter was resolved without bloodshed. I caught up with my wife and the freedmen. "Another hour," I said, "and we'll find a secluded place to rest."

The next day, after a good sleep and an adequate breakfast, we resumed our journey. Both Giscana and Gisco clamored to ride on my horse with me and I let them take turns. We headed northeast along a well-trodden horse path. There were occasional villages, and I would ask farmers in Greek whether the locality was ruled by Carthage or by Rome. When we got to territory that was ruled by Rome, I decided to sell my armor, which identified me as a Carthaginian. I stopped using Carthaginian coins and availed myself of a stash of Roman coins that I had acquired as plunder in Italia. Sometimes there was an inn available, and I would pay for a night's lodging for the seven of us; when there was no inn available we camped by the side of the road. Palonis, Motigon, and I took turns on watch. After about five days of traveling we reached a place where we could see the Mediterranean. We traveled several more days up the coast and were unmolested until we got near to Tarraco.

We were accosted by a group of eight Roman soldiers. "Who are you and where are you going?" their Decurion asked in Latin.

"My Latin is not good," I said, "Do you speak Greek?"

The soldier laughed. "My Greek is not good. Are these your children?"

"Yes," I said. "These are my wife, my children, and two friends."

The men murmured among themselves. "You will come with us," the Decurion said. "We have someone at our camp who speaks Greek. Give us your weapons." I surrendered my sword and dagger, and Palonis and Motigan surrendered their daggers.

He led us to his army camp. It was strange to me to see a functioning Roman military camp. The only ones I had ever been in were those that we had overrun and pillaged. The place was set up with precision: there were straight roads and evenly spaced tents, and it hummed with activity. We were taken to a tent.

"Lucius!" called the Decurion, "We found these strangers on the road heading toward Tarraco. The man doesn't speak much Latin but says he speaks Greek. Can you talk to him in Greek?"

Lucius came out and looked us over. He was a young man, tall and thin, with a trim beard. He didn't seem threatening. He smiled down at Giscana and Gisco.

"Greek? That will be a nice change from speaking Celtiberian," said Lucius in Greek. "Come into my tent. I have a desk and parchment for writing things down." The tent was larger than most and was lit with several oil lamps. In one corner sat a young woman sewing. She did not look up from her work. Lucius pointed to a stool. "Please sit." He sat down behind the desk and took out parchment and stylus.

"Now, who are you, and why are you traveling to Tarraco? Who are the woman and children and these other men?"

"My name is Gisco," I said. "I'm a deserter from the Carthaginian army, and I was coming to Tarraco because it is firmly in Roman control. I bring my wife and three children, and two freedmen."

"The name Gisco sounds Carthaginian," said Lucius, looking amazed. "You're Carthaginian?"

"Yes," I said.

"A Carthaginian deserter!" he exclaimed. "That never happens! The Spanish tribesmen are fickle, and we see deserters from time to time, but an actual Carthaginian? Never. How do we know you're not a spy? You must realize that we Romans believe that there is no such thing as an honest Carthaginian."

"Yes, I know," I said. "I once heard a Roman say, 'Lying is for Carthaginians.' But the Carthaginian army would never send a Carthaginian as a spy. That would be too obvious. We have so many other nationalities in our employ that can blend in much more easily. I was highly placed in the Carthaginian army. I was lieutenant to Mago Barca, the brother of Hannibal, and my brother is Hasdrubal, son of Gisco, the general who leads an army down in Gades. I can offer General Scipio a lot of information."

Young Lucius looked shocked. "I've never heard anything so unbelievable!" he said. "And even if it were all true, you say these things so matter-of-factly. Are you not the least bit ashamed of being a traitor? What is your price for selling information to your enemies?"

"The safety of my wife and children. That is my only price," I said. "Yes, I'm ashamed of being a traitor to my country. Do you think I would do this if I had a choice?"

"What do you mean, if you had a choice?" said Lucius. "Why do you have no choice?"

"Do you see the baby in my wife's arms?" I said. "He was to be sacrificed as a burnt offering to our gods Tanit and Ba-al

Hammon. This was my only way to prevent it. I trade my honor for his safety."

Lucius stared at me open-mouthed for a long moment. "You mean it's true what they say about Carthage? True about the sacrifice of infants?"

I nodded. I was on the verge of tears. No, I admit it. I began to weep. We sat for a long time in silence. Finally, Lucius poured a cup of wine and offered it to me. "Thank you," I said. I took the cup and began to sip from it. Not Falernian, but not bad.

"Let me see the child," said Lucius. He left the tent and bade Sansara to show him the baby. He returned to his desk.

"A beautiful child," he said. "I have a son of my own back in Rome." He shook his head. "I can't understand you Carthaginians. How could you possibly…"

"I couldn't," I said. "That's why I'm here. A traitor with no country."

"Your wife doesn't look Carthaginian," said Lucius.

"Sansara is the granddaughter of the chieftain of the Volciani," I replied. "It was a political match, but she's a good wife and we are happy together."

"What about the two men with you? Who are they?" asked Lucius.

"My freedmen. I set them free but they wouldn't leave," I said. "One is an Iberian Greek, and the other is a Carpetani."

"We will have to investigate this matter further," said Lucius. "We will need to know if you really are who you say you are. I will have to consult with Gneius Scipio when he returns. In the meantime you and your family and freedmen will be held in comfortable confinement in Tarraco. My intuition tells me you are telling the truth, even if you are a Carthaginian." He smiled. He summoned the Decurion and gave him instructions in Latin.

We were taken to a villa in Tarraco where we were confined to a suite of three rooms and kept under guard. Our accommodations were simple, but adequate. The female slaves fussed and cooed over the children and provided Sansara with material and thread so that she could occupy herself with sewing and embroidery. They got permission to allow Sansara and Giscana to participate in their activities. Sansara was happier and more relaxed than I had seen her in months.

"The Romans don't seem as bad as they say," said Sansara. "When that man came out of the tent to look at Hanno, Hanno smiled at him and reached up to grab his finger. I thought; if Hanno is not afraid of him, then I won't be either."

"I hope you are right, Sansara," I said. "We will just have to wait and see. At least we're still alive and not in chains."

I was not as fortunate as Sansara. I was not permitted to leave our rooms, and time weighed on my hands. Palonis and Motigon tried to divert me with stories of their lives both before and after their enslavement. I had never known much about them and was amazed and a little shocked at their stories. "My first master used to beat me when I was too slow, and sometimes he used the whip," said Motigon. He showed me his scars. "I was glad when your father bought me. He was always kind." In turn, I related to them all of the events of my journey with Hannibal. Sometimes we played games or gambled small sums with knucklebones. I must be patient, I thought. Sometimes in my despair I wondered if I had done the right thing, but I had only to look at Hanno's smiling face to know that I had.

## MAGO

I left Hamilcar, son of Mazeus, in charge of our camp, and took a unit to Khart Hadasht. Something was seriously amiss if the priests had decided to revive the practice of child sacrifice, and I decided to get to the bottom of this. Accompanied by about a dozen men, I strode into the temple of Tanit and Ba-al Hammon unannounced and demanded to see Indibal.

If Indibal was shocked to see me, he did not show it. His demeanor displayed no emotion at all. His tone was calm and self-assured as he asked me why I had honored him with a visit.

"I want to know why you are insisting that a child be sacrificed to Tanit," I said. "You know that my father frowned upon that practice and so does Hannibal."

"When this child, Hanno, son of Gisco, was born, his parents brought him to our temple to be blessed, as is the custom," said Indibal. "That very night I saw a vision. This child will die in the fire that destroys Carthage. He will be an old man by then, but if he lives, that will be the fate of Carthage, to be burned to the ground by our enemies. Many babies die in their first few months, and I was hoping that he would die, but since he did not, and actually seemed to thrive, I knew that he must be sacrificed to save Carthage."

"But even if it is the fate of Carthage to be burned by our enemies, why would destroying this child change anything?" I asked.

"It would invalidate my vision," said Indibal. "I fear it is too late now to save Carthage. It would have been a very small sacrifice to prevent a huge destruction of our city and our people. I will not live to see this destruction, nor will you, but now Hanno will. He will be destroyed. Scarcely any will survive."

"So you had an evil vision and you tried to sacrifice a child in order to invalidate the vision," I said. "I would advise you to stop having visions. Child sacrifice is strictly forbidden by my decree, and if you violate this order you will meet the same fate as your victims. I swear by all the gods to that!"

"I have seen your fate, Mago, son of Hamilcar," he replied. "You will not live to see the end of this war, and you will leave no children."

"That doesn't matter," I said. "My fate is in the hands of the gods as is the fate of everyone else. Disobey me, Indibal, and your fate will be in my hands, and it won't be pleasant!" I left without making the customary obeisance. Melqart preserve us from mad old priests!

## SANSARA

I feel safe now, at least safer than I have felt in several weeks. We are housed in a lovely villa with a splendid view of the harbor. There is nearly always a pleasant breeze, and we can smell the sea. We can see fishing boats and war ships in the harbor, and it looks lively with all the men working there. This city was founded by Greeks, and I'm told that there's an agora. I'd love to do some shopping there, but we are not allowed to leave the villa.

The women here are all very nice to me and one of them speaks a language close to mine. She told me that their master had rented the villa to the Roman general Gneius Scipio. She said that their master treats them well, and that they are actually better off than a lot of free women. I am happy to help them with their cooking, cleaning, and sewing, but I don't think I would like to be a slave. If a free woman finds herself in a difficult situation, she can at least go home to her parents as Enidia did. The women here might be treated well now, but if their master died or sold them to a crueler master they would have no recourse.

I try to keep Gisco's spirits up. I know this defection to the Romans is hard on him. He is a man of action who likes to be busy, and now he has nothing to do. He feels bad about leaving Mago and deserting the army. He feels bad about helping the Romans. He doesn't hate the Romans, but they are the enemy, and it galls him that he will have to buy our safety by giving them information. I don't understand why the priest insisted on sacrificing Hanno. Gisco says that the practice of child sacrifice goes back thousands of years in Phoenician culture. The Carthaginians are so sophisticated; they are literate and they engage in commerce all around the Mediterranean Sea. They have material wealth that I couldn't even dream of when I lived in my village. Why do they maintain a practice that even we primitive and savage Volciani would find abhorrent?

GISCO

After a few weeks I was summoned to the *tablinum* of the owner of the *domus*. Lucius was there, and alongside him sat two stern-looking middle-aged men wearing togas. "Gisco, please sit here," said Lucius in Greek.

I sat down. I didn't know whether I should look at these men or avert my eyes. What do the Romans do? I did not know what sort of obeisance a Roman makes to the more powerful. I made no obeisance. I decided to look directly at them because I didn't want to give them the impression that I was a slave. I wanted them to see that I was highborn. Romans respect that. I waited for them to speak.

"I am Publius Cornelius Scipio," said one of the men in Greek. "And this is my brother, Gneius Cornelius Scipio. We hold joint imperium as Proconsuls here in Spain, but I will be the one to question you, as my Greek much surpasses that of my brother." He smiled slightly.

"You seem to have recovered well from your unfortunate encounter at Ticinus," I said. "I watched the whole thing from a hill. You were unhorsed and appeared to be getting badly battered, but then a bold Roman soldier led a cavalry charge down the hill, and they snatched you up. It was incredible. Even we Carthaginians had to admire the man."

"'That 'bold Roman soldier' was my son Publius," said the Proconsul with undisguised pride. "You were at Ticinus?"

"Ticinus, Trebia, Trasimene, and Cannae," I said. "I came over the Alps with Hannibal. I returned to Carthage with Hannibal's brother Mago."

"So you were well placed. Certainly you have much to tell us. But what makes a man become a traitor to his country?"

I looked beseechingly at Lucius. "Lucius has given us his opinion," Said Publius Scipio, "but we want to hear this from you."

"I am trading my honor for the life of my son," I said. "What would a Roman do if he were in my place?"

"A Roman would not have your problem," he said. "Romans seldom practice human sacrifice. It did happen just after Cannae when your Hannibal brought Rome to the brink of madness, but the victims were Greek and Gallic slaves, not our own children. Is that why you Carthaginians use mercenaries? Because you destroy too many of your own children to provide for an army?"

"I don't think so," I said. "Child sacrifice is not that common these days, but the practice persists in low numbers from ancient times. More enlightened leaders, such as the Barcas, seek to discourage it, but they have not forbidden it altogether. I don't know why the priest took it into his head to do this to my son. Carthaginians have a different attitude toward war than Romans. Most would rather not dirty their hands with it and would just as soon leave it to mercenaries."

"That's why you Carthaginians will lose this war," said Proconsul Publius Scipio. "You really have only Hannibal, who, although a supremely able general, is just one man. Once he is killed, captured, dies a natural death, or gives up out of sheer frustration, your mercenaries will be useless. Rome can wait him out. I may not live to see our victory, but my sons will. I have also heard that the government in Carthage is badly divided on whether to support this war. Is that not so?"

"I would not deny that, from what I've seen," I said. "But what would you do if you were in my situation?"

"For either of my sons, Publius or Lucius, I would sacrifice my life," admitted Publius Scipio.

"Sacrificing my life would not help Hanno," I said. "It is my honor I am sacrificing."

He turned to his brother Gneius and asked him something in Latin. Gneius replied and Publius Scipio translated: "A difficult choice. A difficult choice, indeed. But we Scipios need not make that choice. You do and you have. There is no going back. Now we must discuss the consequences."

"Very well," I said. "What are the consequences?"

"We have spies in Mago's camp, and they verify your story," said Publius Scipio. "It seems that it was a bit of a scandal, and Mago was enraged. Unfortunately, Carthaginian soldiers are no match for the priesthood.

"These are our terms. We will find you and your family a small domus in Tarraco. You will get a stipend on which to live comfortably. You and your family will be under our protection. In exchange you will answer any questions we have about Carthaginian military matters and political affairs to the best of your knowledge. You are not to leave Tarraco unless accompanied by our soldiers."

"Your terms are merciful, and I accept them." I said.

"Good," said Publius Scipio. "We will let you rest for now. Lucius will have questions for you tomorrow."

The following afternoon, I was summoned back to the tablinum to meet with Lucius. He requested a decanter of wine and two goblets from a servant. He motioned me to sit, and poured wine for both of us. "These meetings need not be unpleasant for either of us," he said. "Let's just consider this a conversation." I nodded.

"Why do you suppose Hannibal decided to make war on Rome?" he asked. I was amazed that he would ask a question with such an obvious answer.

"Revenge, of course," I answered.

"Revenge for the wrongs suffered by Carthage in the previous war?"

"Yes," I replied.

"And what makes Hannibal believe he can defeat Rome?" he asked.

"Hannibal is the most brilliant general that has ever existed. Rome has witnessed what he is capable of. Do you really think he will fail?"

Lucius smiled. "Hannibal is, indeed, a brilliant general, but he is also a great teacher, and Rome is an apt pupil. We Romans learn fast. Yes, I think that in the long run he will fail. We will learn to beat him at his own game.

"But let's get down to specifics. What do you think Hannibal's plans are?"

"I think that he is trying to isolate Rome as much as possible by making alliances with non-Roman peoples in Italia. I think that he wants to establish a seaport on the coast of Italia where our transports will be protected from the Roman fleet, and I think that he awaits reinforcements from Carthage before going back on the offensive," I said. Lucius wrote down everything I said.

"Does he plan to destroy Rome?" asked Lucius.

"After Cannae, he was willing to make peace with Rome. He sent Carthalo to the city with terms, but the Romans wouldn't admit him into the city."

"And what would those terms have been?" asked Lucius.

"I think they were very similar to the terms imposed upon Carthage by Rome in the last war."

"So the idea is subjugation and humiliation, but not total destruction?" asked Lucius.

I smiled. "Yes, but it would seem that Rome will not tolerate subjugation or humiliation, so ultimately Hannibal will have no other choice than to destroy the city." Lucius merely nodded.

"And his brothers Hasdrubal and Mago, and your brother Hasdrubal, son of Gisco; what are their plans?"

"At this point Mago is protecting the silver mines around the area of the Upper Baetis with some 25,000 troops. My brother Hasdrubal is stationed in the area of Aurinx with another 25,000, and Hasdrubal Barca is recruiting among the various tribes. According to Mago, Hasdrubal Barca wants to raise an army to cross the Alps and join with Hannibal. He has enlisted the Ilergites under Indibilis and Mandonius, and has a strong force of Numidians under the command of Masinissa, son of King Gala of the Massylii," I replied.

"Has he made allies among the Celtiberians?" Lucius asked.

"Hasdrubal doesn't really trust the Celtiberians. He has taken a number of hostages from among them and is keeping them at Khart Hadasht. He thinks he can prevail upon them to remain neutral in the war with Rome."

After a couple hours of this "conversation," Lucius got up to leave. He took out a package and unwrapped it. It contained my sword and dagger, and the daggers of my freedmen. "We are returning your weapons. You and your men will be permitted to walk about in the town, and it is best to have some sort of weapon when you do. There are some rough characters about." He picked up one of the daggers. "Is this yours?" he asked. "It looks like a Roman pugio. There are even Latin letters engraved on the hilt— PVG. Where did you get this?"

"I took this from a Roman soldier I slew at Cannae," I said.

Lucius looked solemn. "My cousin Gaius died at Cannae. Maybe you killed him. I guess I should consider myself fortunate that I wasn't there."

"It's possible that I did," I replied. "I killed scores of Romans on the battlefield that day. But the man I took the pugio from died the following day. He was badly wounded and I killed him as a kindness. I paid for the dagger with a coin that I placed in his mouth so that he could pay the raftsman to cross the Styx."

Lucius smiled grimly. "I wonder who got the better of the exchange."

I laughed. "That depends on whether there really is a raftsman. We won't know until we get there." Then I asked, "Have I told you anything you didn't already know?"

He smiled. "We like to get our information from various sources so that one source confirms another, or, if there is a discrepancy, we can investigate it further. That's how intelligence works. Everything has value. I will be back tomorrow. We will be getting into more specifics about how the Carthaginian military operates. Feel free now to walk about the town, but be here tomorrow afternoon when I come back."

During Lucius's subsequent visits, the questions became more and more specific. I gave him information on specific military personnel in Mago's army, and as much as I knew about who was who in the armies of both Hasdrubals. I gave information about supply routes, weapons manufacture, and whatever I knew about our relations and agreements with the various tribes. I told him as much as I knew about the tribes themselves and their leaders. Lucius had a considerable talent for eliciting information. And I? I had never considered myself talented at anything, but it seemed I had a genuine talent for being a traitor!

After one particularly detailed session Lucius must have noticed my discomfort, and he asked me what I was thinking. "I deserve to be crucified," I said. "I really do."

Lucius replied gently, "Perhaps, Gisco. But your little Hanno did not deserve to be burnt."

## MAGO

Mazeus failed to find Gisco and his family on the road to Tarraco. He and his squadron of twelve men entered Roman-held territory, but after a few encounters with Roman patrols, necessitating hasty retreats, Mazeus decided that the pursuit was not worth the risk.

I am still very worried about the information that Gisco can offer the Romans. Of course, it is entirely possible that the Romans will reject Gisco's proposal or even refuse to listen to it. They might execute him, and enslave his wife and children. The Romans frown upon treason. You never know what they are going to do. Gisco has taken a tremendous risk. He must have been in a state of panic to even consider such a course.

What would I have done if I had been in Gisco's situation? Of course, I am much more powerful than Gisco and would have had the ability to refuse the priest's demands. Did Gisco not believe I could have protected him? Could it be that he still sees me as his childhood playmate and does not comprehend the degree of authority I wield here in Spain?

I suppose I was wrong to say that Gisco has never had an original thought. The problem is that his notions are naïve and simplistic, and not appropriate for someone of his station in life. That's why he could never be a leader of men, like me, or like his brother Drubal. In all these years of war, starting with Arbocola, I have never seen him kill a woman or a child under sixteen, even in a situation like Taurinorum where the command was to kill all of the inhabitants. He busies himself with the men and thinks nobody notices. I have tried to explain to him that male children will grow up to be our enemies, and that women, if left alive, will bear children whom they will teach to be our enemies. He thinks that it is "not manly" to kill women and children. I have always thought that this sort of soft-headed thinking would lead him into disaster, and now it has.

It is too late to stop Gisco now. We will just have to keep our spies in Tarraco on the alert for him. If he surfaces I will send a party to abduct him and bring him back for punishment, but I fear it will be too late to undo the damage he will have done.

## SANSARA

I think I'm pregnant again. We have our own little house now, which is very nice for me, although I miss the women at the villa. That's another disadvantage of being a slave; they can't go anywhere on their own, so they can't visit me. A slave is just not her own person. I really don't envy them. I would have a difficult time visiting them with three little children, so I probably won't be able to see them very often.

Lucius has arranged for us to have a domestic slave. Her name is Lula, and she is an old woman; I think she's in her late sixties or early seventies. She can't do all that much, but she helps me cook, keep the house clean, and watch Hanno and Gisco. I don't expect much of her because she has arthritis and doesn't see very well. I think that the household who owns her wanted to get rid of her without throwing her into the street to fend for herself. She seems very simple, but she's sweet and affectionate.

Giscana and Gisco have made friends with the children next door. Polodoro, the man next door, is a sculptor, and the children love to watch him work. I have warned them not to touch any of his tools or materials. His wife, Delgadina, is very nice, and I have picked up enough of the local dialect that we can communicate somewhat. She and I go to the agora together while Lula watches the children. The agora is not impressive compared to the markets of Carthage, or even those of Khart Hadasht, but all of the necessities of life are available and not too expensive. I try not to spend money except on necessities, because we are no longer rich. Gisco no longer has access to his father's money. Gisco says that we will have to spend money on tutors for the children, so we need to be careful. Delgadina knows how to bargain at the agora, so I just do what she does and try to get the best prices. The Romans provide us with enough money to live on, and I have a cache of jewelry we can sell if need be.

I wasn't sure what to tell Delgadina when she asked me what Gisco did for a living. Gisco told me to tell people we were from

Sicily and that he was of Phoenician descent but a Roman subject. Finally, I told her that he translates Phoenician documents for the Romans.

Gisco seems more relaxed now that we have our own place to live. He has shaved off his beard and taken to wearing Greek clothing. I think he looks good without the beard.

I told Gisco I wanted to learn to read, and he bought me a wax tablet and a stylus just like those Giscana has. Giscana is already reading very well, and she is helping me learn. The letters in Phoenician can also represent numbers, so I am learning to count, add, and subtract. I think I'm the first person in my tribe to learn to read and write.

## GISCO

Sansara was pregnant again. If I was ambivalent about what I had done, she certainly was not. She was aware of my discomfort, and every day she expressed her gratitude to me for saving Hanno. Nearly every day she made a point of telling me about something new that little Hanno had accomplished and how beautiful he was and how delighted she was with him.

After some weeks we had pretty much exhausted my store of knowledge about Carthaginian military affairs, and Lucius reduced his visits to one brief pro forma session a week. Sometimes he would ask my opinion on some aspect of Punic culture. We would have discussions about the similarities and differences between our respective civilizations.

"The Scipios are interested to know about your Carthaginian gods," said Lucius one day.

My hand shook and I spilled my wine. "*Cac!*" exclaimed Lucius as he leapt up quickly to get out of the way of the spill. In so doing he knocked over a stool. I preferred any other topic to discussing the gods!

Giscana heard the commotion and ran to get Sansara, who cleaned up the mess with a cloth. I poured myself another cup of wine.

"I'm sorry, Lucius," I apologized.

"Did I say something wrong?" asked Lucius.

"You must realize that I'm 'accursed of the gods,'" I said. "At least that's what the priest of Ba-al Hammon and Tanit told me when I left to come here. I denied them a sacrifice, and I fear they will have their revenge."

"Personally, Gisco, I think that sort of sacrifice is a bit much for any god to demand!" said Lucius. "Why do you think they demand such a thing?"

"I'm a soldier," I said, "not a priest. My father would have preferred that I become a merchant or a priest, but my close friendship with Mago Barca drew me into the military. My brother told me I wasn't suited for military life, and perhaps he was right. I found discomforts there that were not just matters of physical hardship. But, as far as human sacrifice is concerned, I can only say that sacrificing your child is the greatest and most painful of sacrifices, so the gods must value such a thing above all else a human being can do. The priest told me that sacrificing Hanno would save Carthage. If that were so, it would have been the noblest thing I could have done, but I couldn't do it. Besides, I would have been sacrificing more than Hanno; my wife would have turned against me and turned the children against me. I would have lost everything dear to me."

"The priest said your sacrifice would save Carthage?" asked Lucius, "But how?"

"Indibal didn't explain that to me," I replied. "He just expected me to take his word for it."

"So Tanit and Ba-al Hammon are your chief gods? Like Jupiter and Juno?" asked Lucius.

"You might say that," I said. "Our other gods don't demand human sacrifice, so you might say they are cheaper gods. The Barcas are devoted to the god Melqart. Melqart is something like your Hercules. Before Hannibal invaded Italy he made a pilgrimage to Melqart's temple at Gades and made sacrifices there. His brothers Hasdrubal and Mago accompanied him, and my brother and I went as well. Besides Melqart, we also have Ishtar, a goddess of fertility borrowed from the Cretans, and Eshmoun, a god of healing, something like the Greek god Aesculapius."

"So I take it that you favor the god Melqart over Ba-al Hammon and Tanit," said Lucius.

I smiled. "Yes, especially now that I have experienced Tanit's evil nature. Melqart is a good god for a soldier. There are many gods. One can choose which to worship, and I choose not to worship a god that would have me sacrifice my child. But even if

I ignore these gods, I don't know whether they will ignore me, or whether they will seek retribution."

"We Romans have many gods as well," said Lucius. "And if Melqart is like Hercules, I agree that he's a good god for a soldier. He's my favorite god as well; whenever I swear, I swear by Hercules. I also pray to be favored by the goddess Fortuna, but Fortuna is known to be fickle."

"I have also heard you swear by Edepol," I said. "What god is that?"

Lucius laughed. "That's a short form of 'by Castor and Pollux.'"

"But aren't those Greek gods?" I asked.

"We Romans have borrowed, or stolen, if you will, all manner of gods from the Greeks." Lucius replied. "Sometimes we have changed the names. The Greek Poseidon is our Neptune, Zeus is Jupiter, Hera is Juno, Athena is Minerva, Ares is Mars and Aphrodite is Venus. Sometimes we don't bother to change the name. Apollo is Apollo."

"But you can see why I'm afraid of gods," I said. "I have defied the gods Tanit and Ba-al Hammon, and I fear that they will destroy me."

"Perhaps you can pray to Melqart to protect you from them," suggested Lucius.

The Romans found us a small house and posted a guard there. They told me that this was for our protection. There was an atrium, a kitchen, a small tablinum and three bedrooms, one for Sansara and me, one for the children, and one for the guard. We were allotted the services of an elderly female slave named Lula, who helped Sansara with domestic chores. She slept in the room with the children. The domus was in an area of that city that was inhabited mostly by craftsmen and small shopkeepers. The next-door neighbor, Polodoro, was a sculptor. He and his wife were friendly, and Giscana and Gisco loved to watch him work. They spent much of their time playing with the couple's three children, who were all under seven. Sansara and Polodoro's wife, Delgadina, soon became close friends.

I was permitted to wander freely through the city. Tarraco had been founded by Greeks, and most of the population spoke Greek, so I had little trouble communicating with people. I started going to a barber and having my beard shaved regularly, which, I hoped, would make it more difficult for Carthaginian agents to recognize me. I also dressed in Greek style rather than Carthaginian. I would go to the public baths on most days, and often I would go to one of the taverns to have a drink and to see if I could overhear talk of what was going on with the war. Sometimes I would join in low-stakes gambling games. I got to know some of the locals and made a few friends. Some people were curious about me.

"You're not from here, Gisco," said Herodion, the tavern owner. "Where do you come from? You look and talk like a Phoenician."

Obviously, I didn't want to reveal who I really was, so I said, "I'm from Lilybaeum, in Sicily. It used to be a Phoenician city before the last war between Rome and Carthage, but it's been ruled by Rome since. I'm Phoenician by descent, but, like all of you, a subject of Rome."

"So who do you hope will win this war?" Herodion persisted.

I shrugged. "It doesn't much matter," I said. "What I'd really like to see is a lasting peace." My answers seemed to satisfy my new neighbors and I sensed no animosity from them.

It was myself that I could not satisfy. How difficult it is to shake off the teachings and loyalties implanted in youth. In my heart I still loved Carthage, I still loved Aba and Uma and Buba. I still loved Mago. Even as I served the Romans, in my heart I still wanted Carthage to win the war. Yet I knew my past life was lost forever. There was no going back, and I grieved for what I had lost. All I had now was Sansara and the children. They were wonderful in themselves, and I would have to be content with what I had.

I tried to spend time every day with Giscana and Gisco, and started teaching them both to read and write in Phoenician and Greek. Thinking that they should also become literate in Latin, I hired a tutor for them, and, since I thought that it would be good idea for me to learn Latin, I paid him to tutor me as well. After about a year I could carry on a conversation. I made a point of practicing my Latin with Lucius when he came by. Sometimes my pronunciation had him doubling over with laughter.

Noticing Sansara's condition on one of his visits Lucius asked me, "Have you made arrangements for a midwife?"

"I've been worried about that," I replied. "I was just thinking I'd have to do it myself, with maybe a little assistance from Lula. But I've never delivered a baby before."

"Why don't I send my woman servant, Ala," he said, "she knows something about delivering babies."

"That would be a big help," I said. "I'm surprised they let you have a woman servant in your camp. I thought Roman military camps were off-limits to women."

"They make an exception for Ala because Gneius Scipio wanted me to learn Celtiberian and she teaches me," said Lucius. "Anyway, she dislikes men and never leaves the tent without me or my groom Brunius to accompany her, so she's really no problem in the camp. Give her a nice piece of jewelry as payment. She has a fondness for jewelry."

When Sansara went into labor I sent Palonis to notify Lucius, and he brought Ala to our house. She was as Lucius had described. She would have been attractive, but she had a wary and suspicious demeanor about her, and I could believe that she disliked men. She got along well enough with Sansara; their languages were close enough that they could communicate somewhat, and after several hours in labor, Sansara delivered a son, whom we named Himilco. I let Ala select a couple of pieces from Sansara's stash of jewelry.

Where Hanno had been smiling and quiet, Himilco was lusty and loud. He was difficult to comfort, and Sansara thought that he might have colic.

Tarraco came to seem like an island of tranquility in a sea of war, death, and destruction. Palonis and Motigon found employment as stevedores in the dockyards. They rented a room not far from us. They worked hard but enjoyed life when not working. They seemed uninterested in women, and I suspected that they satisfied each other's needs.

Tarraco was a seaport that had started out as a fishing village. Some of the friends I made while frequenting the baths and the taverns were fishermen, and one day, one of them, a man named Demetrios, invited me to come fishing with him. He taught me his techniques for catching fish and I found I enjoyed the activity. I started going out on his boat once or twice a week, fishing for tuna and mullet. I would take one or two fish home for Sansara to cook, and give Demetrios the rest of my catch, so he did not mind bringing me at all. When little Gisco turned five, I started bringing him along.

Nearly four years passed of this pleasant, if pointless, existence. Then one day Lucius came by to see me.

"You won't be seeing me for a while." he said. "The Scipios are planning a major offensive, and I will be going with Gneius. This whole venture may take several months."

"Try to stay safe," I said. "If I don't see you again, I want you to know that I have appreciated your kindness. When I first came to your tent, I feared that I would be crucified or enslaved. There was no compelling reason for you to believe my story."

"I had only to look at the child," said Lucius. "Men lie, but babies don't."

Then he added "I'm just curious, Gisco; I've never asked you this, but is it true that the Carthaginians crucify their own generals when they lose a battle?"

"Not these days, but it did happen in the last war." I said.

"We Romans don't do that," Lucius said. "Even after Cannae, Gaius Terentius Varro was not punished. He still leads legions in Italy. In the last war Claudius Pulcher lost 93 ships and was only mildly punished. But how do you Carthaginians get anyone to volunteer to be a general if they know they could be crucified for losing a battle?"

"As I said, things have changed." I said. "I don't think Hannibal or any of the Carthaginian generals in this war have anything to fear. The Barca faction is just too powerful in Carthage. My own grandfather was crucified, but it was at the hands of the rebellious mercenaries after the war. They hadn't been paid in a timely fashion because Carthage was depleted by the war, and they kept increasing their demands. They captured my grandfather Gisco and crucified what remained of him after they dismembered him. My grandmother mourns him to this day. Hannibal's father Hamilcar put down the rebellion and the rebels met cruel deaths."

"You don't suppose the same thing could happen again if Carthage is defeated, do you?" asked Lucius.

"I certainly hope not. The mercenary war was cruel and brutal beyond measure," I said. "But Hannibal's soldiers are devoted to him, and I know that Mago maintains good relations with his men. I could see something like that happening with my brother's mercenaries, though."

"I gather you're not that fond of your brother," said Lucius.

"No, we've pretty much been at odds since early childhood," I said. "That's why I didn't serve under him. I always found Mago much more compatible."

"I'm not close to my brothers either; they were much older than me and pretty much ignored me," said Lucius. "They were actually half-brothers from my father's first marriage."

Lucius got up to leave. "Farewell," I said, "and thank you again for everything you've done for us."

He smiled. "Perhaps we'll meet again, Gisco; if not in this world, then in Hades."

MAGO

Our spies in Tarraco have informed us that the Scipios are planning a mobilization against us. I went to an emergency meeting in Khart Hadasht with my brother Hasdrubal, and with Hasdrubal, son of Gisco. Also attending the meeting were Masinissa, the Prince of the Massylii who leads our force of mounted Numidians; Indibilis and his brother Mandonius, the leaders of our northern allies, the Ilergites; and a Celtiberian in our employ named Gorgo.

"Gorgo," said my brother, "how much gold will you need to pay Gneius Scipio's mercenaries not to fight?"

Gorgo laughed. "I would pay them twice what they are promised from the Romans. Who wouldn't be pleased with a deal like that? Twice the gold for doing nothing and not putting your life at risk on behalf of people you don't care about!"

"So the Celtiberians are not all that loyal to the Romans?" asked my brother.

"Celtiberians are loyal to whomever pays us more," said Gorgo, "something to bear in mind any time you are tempted to stint on our pay. Celtiberians couldn't care less about who wins this war. Personally, I favor Carthage. One of the Romans has stolen my stepdaughter, and that brings me to my other offer. This Roman serves Gneius Scipio as his liaison with the spies who bring him information from the various tribes. He knows everything about the tribes, who is loyal to the Romans, and what their treaties and secret arrangements are. His name is Lucius Varro and he has a wealth of information you could use to weed out pro-Roman influences among the tribes of Spain. For a thousand *shekels* I will capture him and bring him to you alive so that you can extract this information."

"Very well, Gorgo," said my brother. "We agree to your terms. But you don't get the thousand shekels for the man until you bring him to us."

"One more thing," said Gorgo, "This Lucius handles both spies and deserters, and we believe that there is a highly ranked Carthaginian deserter in Tarraco whom he has been interviewing."

I turned my gaze toward Hasdrubal, son of Gisco, and he returned my stare. We were both thinking the same thing.

"Try to find out who this man is and where he is located," said my brother. "Another thousand shekels if your information leads to his capture." Gorgo nodded and then continued.

"My twenty thousand Celtiberian mercenaries will be attached to Gneius Scipio's forces. Once they desert, he will be left with only 10,000 Roman foot soldiers and 600 horse. The plan is that Publius Scipio will bring a force of 20,000 Roman foot soldiers and 1,200 horse soldiers to attack Hasdrubal Barca's army, while Gneius and his 10,000 Romans and 20,000 Celtiberian mercenaries will come after the armies of Mago Barca and Hasdrubal, son of Gisco. My advice would be to bring the Illergites and Masinissa's Numidians to bear against Publius. Once you destroy him you can easily rout the ten thousand Romans who will remain with Gneius Scipio after my men desert."

My brother smiled. "Thank you for your information and for your assistance, Gorgo. If all goes as planned, you will soon be the wealthiest man of your tribe. If you can bring the Celtiberian tribes to our side, Carthage will support you in any effort you may make to become chieftain over all the Celtiberians."

After the meeting we had a feast. Masinissa seated himself next to Gisco's brother Drubal. He said to Drubal, "Would you consider a marital alliance between your family and mine? I have seen your daughter, and she promises to be quite a beauty. I would be delighted to take her for my wife."

"The child's not ready for marriage yet, Masinissa. She's only eleven, and I'm sure her mother wouldn't want to part with her for a few years," replied Drubal.

"For a prize like Caphonbal, I would certainly be willing to wait three or four more years," said Masinissa.

Drubal smiled. "I will think about it, Masinissa. Bring me the head of Publius Cornelius Scipio and I will certainly think about it."

Masinissa grinned and picked up his goblet of wine. "To our success in the coming battle!" he proclaimed.

Masinissa could never sit still for very long, and was soon lured away by a comely slave girl. I took his place on the couch beside Drubal. "Do you think that the highly ranked Carthaginian deserter whom Gorgo was talking about is your brother?" I asked.

Drubal nodded. "Little doubt of it; who else would it be? What other Carthaginian soldier has ever deserted to the Romans?" He shook his head and frowned.

"What would you have done if it had been your son Bomilcar that the priest demanded for sacrifice?" I asked him.

"Me? I would have killed the priest, or failing that, commandeered a ship to take us to Carthage," replied Drubal. "I would never dream of taking refuge with the Romans! What do you intend to do to Gisco when you capture him?"

"He'll be crucified as a traitor," I said. "I feel bad about it because we were friends for so long, but this sort of thing cannot go unpunished." Frankly, I couldn't envision Gisco killing the priest or commandeering a ship, but I didn't mention that to Drubal.

"Yes, that is the right thing to do," said Drubal. "I will leave the matter in your hands. I will not pursue the matter, because my parents would be appalled if I committed fratricide. As far as I'm concerned, his execution is best left to his commanding officer. What about his wife and children?"

"We still have to maintain good relations with his wife's grandfather, the chieftain of the Volciani," I said, "and I'm sure your parents would not want their grandchildren killed. I will be merciful to them."

"I see your point," said Drubal. "Send them to my parents. I don't want to take responsibility for them. My wife doesn't care for Sansara. I think she's jealous of her youth and beauty," he smiled ruefully. "Better to keep the two of them apart."

## GISCO

Several weeks after Lucius left, there were sounds of mourning and lamentation throughout the city. We received word that the Roman forces, both those of Publius Scipio and those of Gneius, had been nearly wiped out. First Publius had fallen, and then, a few weeks later, Gneius. Personally, I was amazed. I really didn't think Mago and the two Hasdrubals had this in them. Apparently they had had considerable luck on their side. The Scipios had divided their forces. Publius had attacked the Illergites, but then Masinissa's Numidian cavalry and Mago's infantry ambushed them and nearly wiped them out. Gneius had ill fortune of another sort. He had hired 20,000 Celtiberian mercenaries. Hasdrubal Barca's agents paid them not to fight and they left the battle. Masinissa and Mago, having finished with Publius Scipio's army, went after Gneius Scipio and pretty much completed the job. I had little hope that Lucius had survived.

I considered what to do. We had limited resources and no safe place to go. I suspected that Mago knew that I was here, and that if he or my brother took the town, I would be recognized and would end up staring into the eyes of Memon. What would happen to Sansara and the children?

Some three weeks after we received these ill tidings there was a knock on the door. "Lucius!" I exclaimed. "You're alive! I'm so glad to see you!" Lucius looked gaunt and exhausted, and his right hand was wrapped in a bandage, but he seemed otherwise unharmed.

"I'm glad to see you too, Gisco," said Lucius. "I was lucky to make it back here alive. We were nearly wiped out. We have about 8,000 survivors out of some 32,000 Roman troops that were in Spain. We have fortified our camp and elected a general from among ourselves. His name is Lucius Marcius. I've come tell you that we have received news that both Mago and your brother Hasdrubal have crossed the Iberus with their armies and are headed toward our camp. Obviously we can no longer provide you with any protection. I have to take your guard, Manilius, away with me because we need every soldier we can get. I tell you this so that you can take whatever measures you see fit to protect yourself and your family."

"Thank you for the information, Lucius," I said. "I'm at a loss as to what to do. Sansara is near term with the baby so it would not be convenient to travel right now. After she delivers, perhaps we can take a ship to Sicily. As a Phoenician, I might fit in in Lilybaeum."

"That's a thought, Gisco," said Lucius. "If I don't see you again, may the gods be with you." We embraced and he left, accompanied by the guard.

Attended by Delgadina and Lula, Sansara delivered a little girl. We named her Elissa after the founder of Carthage. Giscana was thrilled to finally have a little sister. She did everything she could to help her mother.

I decided to look into the possibility of taking my family to Lilybaeum. I worried that the armies of Mago and both Hasdrubals might unite and drive the Romans from Spain once and for all. If this happened, I might be discovered and meet a dreadful fate. Demetrios told me that I was more likely to find a vessel sailing to Sicily from Emporion than from Tarraco. I had sold three of the four horses we had taken from Khart Hadasht, and had boarded the fourth in a local stable. I decided to ride northward to Emporion.

In Emporion I found that there would be a merchant vessel sailing to Sicily in three weeks. I inquired as to whether there would be room for me, Sansara, and the five children. The captain told me there would be, and I paid him a deposit.

# TWELVE

## ABDUCTED

MAGO
211 B.C.

We are victorious at last! Both Publius and Gneius Scipio are dead and their armies all but annihilated. It only remains for us to cross the Iberus and destroy the remnants. Drubal, son of Gisco, and I will both bring our armies. It was a glorious battle! Publius Scipio's men attacked the Ilergites, but Masinissa's Numidian horsemen and my infantry came to their rescue, and by nightfall we had wiped out nearly all of the enemy; very few escaped. We found the body of Publius Scipio on the battlefield, still wrapped in his bright red cloak, a spear shaft protruding from his heart. I don't know why Roman Consuls and Proconsuls insist on wearing red on the battlefield—it makes them such obvious targets! Roman hubris, I suppose.

Once we had disposed of Publius Scipio's army, we went after Gneius Scipio. He had hired 20,000 mercenaries from among the Celtiberians, but he didn't know that we had an agent among them, and that my brother, Hasdrubal, paid the agent to keep his men out of the battle. Why fight and risk your life, when you will get paid just as much to stand aside? Gneius Scipio's loyal Roman forces numbered only about 10,000 and could not hold out against our combined army of 50,000.

My brother Hasdrubal will try to get word of our great victory to Hannibal. This will please him greatly. Once we clear the last remaining Romans from northern Spain, Hasdrubal will bring an army over the Alps to join Hannibal, and we will finish this war once and for all. I think that Hannibal was unwise to seek to make peace with Rome after Cannae—we must destroy Rome. Now that we have virtually all of Spain securely in our hands, it will be possible. Who do the Romans have that they can spare to reconquer Spain? Who would want to go up against our combined armies? Surely this battle, the battle of the Upper Baetis, will be the turning point in this long war.

One of the benefits of our victory is that Castulo and Iliturgis and several other cities that had been allied with the Romans have come back into our alliance. This will make Hannibal's wife, Imilce, happy, because now she can go and visit her parents in Castulo. I visited Iliturgis myself a few days after the battle to cement our alliance, and they proudly displayed a score or so of Roman heads on pikes. The poor bastards had escaped the battle and sought refuge there, thinking that the town was still friendly to Rome. Soon, if we have our way, there will be no safe place for a Roman anywhere in Spain.

My spies report that they have discovered the whereabouts of Gisco. He is living in Tarraco. He has no apparent occupation, so he must still be in the pay of the Romans. That's a bit of unfinished business that I feel obligated to undertake, much as it gives me no joy. I will hire some of Indibilis's men for the task.

## SANSARA

The men came to the house while Gisco was away in Emporion trying to find transportation for us to Sicily. Gisco told me that he didn't think we were safe here in Tarraco, and, unfortunately, he was right.

"You are the wife of Gisco, son of Gisco," said their leader in awkward Phoenician. "You and your children will come with us. You are subjects of Carthage and we have orders to bring you back to Carthaginian territory. You will pack your clothes, blankets, and any food you have on hand."

"Who gave you these orders?" I asked.

"I cannot tell you that, but the orders come from very high up. You will do exactly what we tell you, wife of Gisco."

The men were heavily armed with swords and spears, and I was not about to defy them. I did not know what tribe they were from or what language they spoke. I called Lula to help me pack, but she was almost useless. She began to blubber and weep. I put my arm around her.

"Please, Lula, stop crying. You'll upset the children."

She was like a child. "Sansara, my lady, I don't want you to go," she sniffed. "Please don't go!"

"I don't have a choice, Lula. You see they have swords. Now help me. We can't keep them waiting or they might do us harm."

"Giscana," I said, "put your clothes in a sack and help me and Lula with your brothers' clothes."

"Mama," said Giscana, "Where are they taking us? Are they going to hurt us?"

"Hush, darling, I don't know," I replied. "We have to do what they say. Don't frighten the boys."

"I want to bring the statue Polodoro gave me!" cried Hanno.

"Yes, dear, bring it," I said. Hanno had developed a fascination for carvings and statues from watching Polodoro work. Polodoro had given him a miniature statue of a faun.

Finally we were packed and we climbed into the wagon. Lula stood by the door, weeping once again. I held the baby, Elissa, on one knee, and Himilco on the other. The children were shocked and silent. Hanno clutched his statue, Giscana hugged her rag doll, and little Gisco sucked his thumb. I had weaned Himilco but now I let him nurse from my breast to comfort him. I was afraid, though, that I would run out of milk for Elissa. Every few hours our captors stopped the cart and let us out to walk around for a few minutes and relieve ourselves. After our own food was used up, they gave us two meals a day from their own stores.

Day after day, the wagon, drawn by two horses, made its way south toward Carthaginian territory. Who sent these men? I wondered. What would they do to us? Would we be crucified or would they grant us a merciful death? A people who would sacrifice infants as burnt offerings could not be expected to show mercy to the wife and children of a traitor. For the sake of the children I forced myself to remain calm. It would only make things worse for all of us if I gave in to despair and panic. I could face my death with dignity, but, by all the gods, I hoped that they would not make me watch as they murdered my children!

"I don't like it here, Mama," said little Gisco. "I want to go home!"

"I know, Gisco," I said. "I want to go home too, but these men say we have to go with them. Do you want to hear a story?"

"Yes, Mama, Tell us a story."

I started telling them all the stories I learned as a child in my village. I told them all about the different people in my village, and the story about how I came to Khart Hadasht to marry their father. And when I was done, I told the same stories again. Little children don't seem to mind that.

Every day I scratched a mark on the wood of the cart with a stone. It was after nine days that we reached a Carthaginian military camp. We were taken to a tent, guarded by soldiers.

## MAGO

The cart bearing Gisco's wife Sansara and their children arrived today. She had left Khart Hadasht with three children, and now she had five! Gisco must have had plenty of time on his hands.

The Ilergites brought them to my tent. She was nursing the youngest, an infant girl, and the two-year-old boy was clinging to her robes whining for her attention. The oldest child, a girl, took the little boy by the hand and asked me, in perfect Phoenician, if she could take the child for a walk. I nodded. The two other boys sat quietly, holding hands.

"Sansara," I said. "Do you need a translator?"

"No," she answered. "I speak Phoenician every day with Gisco and the children."

"You and the children will not be harmed," I assured her. "I would not offend your grandfather. We will send you to Carthage, where you can live with Gisco's parents.

"And Gisco?" she asked.

"Gisco must die." I said, "He is a traitor to Carthage."

"You call Gisco a traitor?" her eyes blazed with a fervor that shocked me. "What sort of man stands by and watches his own son burn? If Gisco had done that, he would have been far worse than a traitor, and I would have killed him myself, for that is what he would have deserved! You Phoenicians burn your own children, and you dare to call us, the Volciani, savages! When the Romans came to my grandfather to ask for an alliance, he rebuked them for failing to defend their own allies, the Saguntines. What will my grandfather think now of his alliance with the Carthaginians when you destroy my Gisco for what he had to do to save his son from the fire?"

"I am sorry, Sansara," I said, "but I must do my duty."

"Then kill me too," She said. "I will not be able to control my behavior when Gisco dies. Remember, I am a savage. I take no responsibility for what I may destroy."

The Greeks have a word for this sort of thing: hysteria. It made me even more grateful that Enidia, my Turditani wife, went back to her people. You can never tell what one of these tribal women might do.

"Listen, Sansara," I said. "I don't like this any better than you do. Gisco was my friend. He saved my life at the battle of Trebia."

"Then, Mago," she said, "you owe him a life. Such a debt must be paid."

I had not thought of this, but she was right. Did I have the courage to do the right thing? Was it even within my power?

"Very well, Sansara," I said, "I don't know if I can save Gisco. Treason is a serious crime. I'll do what I can."

"That's all I ask of you, Mago," she said. "Only your brothers Hannibal and Hasdrubal have more power than you, and they are not here, so Gisco's fate is in your hands. Remember your debt to him."

"You and the children will leave tomorrow for Carthage, I said. "I wish you a safe journey."

## SANSARA

We have arrived in Carthage after a three-day journey at sea. We were escorted by two Carthaginian military triremes and, fortunately, had no encounters with the Romans. Giscana, Hanno, and I got seasick, but little Gisco seemed to have no ill effects. I suppose this was because he was used to boats from having gone fishing so many times with his father. I was glad I wasn't pregnant or it would have been worse.

When we got to the quay, the captain sent a messenger to Gisco's father and he came down to meet us. Giscana did not remember him, and the other children had never met him, but he seemed delighted to see us. He patted my shoulder and said, "It's so nice to see you again, Sansara. You're prettier than ever. And this must be Giscana; such a big grown-up girl! And so pretty, just like her Uma!"

Then he looked over the other children. "You must be Gisco and you must be Hanno! Gisco looks just like his Aba and Hanno looks like his Uma! We are going to have great fun together!

"Tell me, Gisco and Hanno, what do you want to be when you grow up?"

Gisco replied, "I want to be a fisherman," and Hanno said, "I want to be a sculptor!"

Aba started laughing as though this were the funniest thing he had ever heard.

"Why do you laugh, Grandfather?" asked little Gisco, frowning. Hanno also looked puzzled.

"A fisherman! A sculptor! Oh my!" Aba shook his head. "Those are honorable occupations, but those are occupations for poor people. Carthaginians of our class become merchants, priests, or army officers. I'm going to have both of you educated, and then you can choose an appropriate occupation. You can still fish or sculpt as hobbies, but fishing and sculpting are not suitable occupations for well-born Carthaginians. Someday, Gisco, you will be wealthy and can buy yourself a fishing boat and fish for fun during your free time, or you can buy a whole fleet of them and hire people to fish for you and sell the fish for a profit. And you, Hanno, may someday build a workshop and have people make sculptures for you that you can sell for a profit. The important thing is that you are the boss and you are the one who makes the profit."

"But I like to carve," said Hanno. "I don't want anyone doing it for me. When I grow up I will be the best sculptor in the world!"

Aba laughed. "When you're rich you can spend your time doing anything you choose. You can spend as much time carving as you like. But first you have to get rich and you won't get rich by making sculptures." Hanno thought about this for a few minutes and then said, "Very well, I'll get rich first and then I will become the best sculptor in the world."

Aba hired litters to take us to his mansion in Megara, and I realized that my children were about to discover what it meant to be rich.

## GISCO

When I returned to Tarraco I found the house empty. It looked as if it had been ransacked. Sansara and all five children were gone! I called out "Sansara! Sansara!" I heard sobs coming from the kitchen and found Lula huddled in a corner weeping. It was difficult to get anything intelligible out of her since she was an Iberian tribeswoman who spoke little Greek or Latin. Between sobs she said "Men. Men take Sansara and children." Then several men came to the door and barged in. They were on top of me before I could draw my sword. They bound me in chains, put a gag in my mouth and a blindfold around my eyes. They did not bother with the old slave woman, who had the intelligence to remain silent and withdraw from the room. From what I had seen of them and from what I could hear of their speech, I suspected that they were Ilergites, Indibilis's men, sent by one of the Carthaginian generals, Hasdrubal Barca, Mago, or my brother Drubal, to bring me back for punishment.

I lay there helpless for what seemed forever. At some point I had no choice but to urinate in my garments. No one offered me food or drink. When night came they picked me up, carried me out to a wagon, and lifted me into it. After a few minutes, I began to feel the motion of the wheels underneath. The road was rough and I was constantly jostled. This was not going to be a pleasant journey. The prospect of being nailed to a cross at the end of it made it even less so. I thought about my life. I was thirty-two. I shouldn't complain, I thought; many men these days don't even make it this far. I could only hope that my captors would show mercy to Sansara and the children and not punish them for my crimes, but I wasn't at all confident about that. I would be crucified for treason. There would be no mercy for me.

I hoped I would die before we got to our destination, but it wasn't to be. The next day the wagon made a stop and my captors removed my chains, the gag, and the blindfold. They took my expensive but soiled robes and gave me a slave's tunic to wear. Then they placed a pot of water and a piece of bread before me, and their leader said. "eat," in badly pronounced Phoenician. I shook my head and he produced a small knife and made it clear that if I didn't eat he would shove the point under my fingernails. I nodded and began to eat and drink. Evidently they were being paid to bring me back alive. There's no point in crucifying a dead man. I've heard, though, that some years ago they actually did crucify a dead man, one Mago, who had lost a battle against the Greeks and had committed suicide to avoid crucifixion. I would have to say that I would rather be crucified dead than crucified alive. After I ate they replaced the chains and we traveled until dusk. I could tell from the position of the sun that we were heading south. I did not have the temerity to ask them who they were or where they were taking me. I remained silent and they asked me no questions.

After a few days we reached the Iberus, which was the border of Roman territory. The wagon came to a halt before a stone bridge. There was a Roman guard at the bridge. One of the Ilergites came into the wagon, sat beside me, and held a dagger to my neck. "Romans," he said. "One word and you're a dead man." I nodded.

The Roman guard asked my captors in Latin why they were transporting a man in chains.

"Escaped slave," replied one of the Ilergites. "We take him back to his master."

The Roman addressed me but I just stared at him blankly, pretending I didn't understand Latin. I don't know what would have happened if I had said something. Would the Ilergites have dared to kill me in front of the Romans? I was too dispirited to try to find out. Later I asked myself whether I would have been better off if I had spoken to the Roman in Latin and provoked my captors to kill me. I regretted my failure to do that.

After about ten days, we reached a Carthaginian military camp. I recognized the camp as Mago's, located north of Castulo. The last time I was here I was an honored and respected officer and everyone scrambled to obey my commands. Now I was a prisoner in chains, dressed in a slave's tunic. I heard a voice say, "You have him. Very good. Did he give you any trouble?"

"Do you think we would let him give us trouble?" replied a man in heavily accented Phoenician. "It was five to one. We had him silenced and immobilized immediately."

"Good. Take him to the general's tent and then you can go to the paymaster and get your money."

They took me to a tent. After ten days of meager diet and no mobility, I could barely walk. Once inside, I fell to my knees.

"Gisco." I recognized Mago's voice. I looked up at him but said nothing. He stared at me intently. He sent the Illergites off to receive their bounty and instructed his servants: "Remove his chains, feed him, give him a bath and a clean robe. I'll talk to him in the morning."

I was surprised by this kind treatment, but I knew that I would be questioned about my activities during the past four years and would be held accountable for them. After the ordeal of the journey I was weak, exhausted, and nearly beyond caring. The only thing I worried about was the fate of Sansara and the children. After I was fed and bathed, I was taken to a tent and I fell asleep immediately.

I slept soundly but I awakened at first light. When the veil of sleep lifted and I realized where I was and contemplated the fate that awaited me, the full force of the terror I had been suppressing took hold of me. I could feel my heart pounding. I felt so cold that I began to shiver. I must not give in to this panic, I thought. Today the god Ba-al Hammon and the goddess Tanit will exact their revenge for my defiance. But curse them! I will defy them to the end. I did the right thing and I will go to my death with my self-respect intact.

Guards appeared at the entrance to the tent. I was given breakfast and brought to Mago's tent. He sat at a small desk covered with maps and reports. I made no obeisance, as such a gesture could be interpreted as pleading for my life, and there was no point in doing that. He didn't appear to be offended. He motioned me to a stool and I sat down, staring at him in silence.

"Gisco," he said, "Have you nothing to say? Have you forgotten how to speak Phoenician?"

"Would it do me any good to beg you not to harm my wife and children?" I asked.

"I can see that you love your wife and children more than anything else," he said. "You love them more than you love your country."

"I can't deny something I've already proven," I said, "but my wife and children are innocent. This was my decision and I take full responsibility for my offense."

"You know it doesn't work that way, Gisco," said Mago. "The innocent are often made to suffer for the crimes of their relatives. Do you remember Dasius, the turncoat who sold us the granary in Clastidium for 400 gold pieces?"

I nodded.

"He later went back to the Romans under Fabius, and offered to restore the city of Arpi to them. The Romans took him into custody. He left his wife and children in Bruttium, and Hannibal made an example of him by summoning them to his camp and crucifying them, then setting them afire as they hung from the crosses."

His words stunned me into silence. I had nothing more to say. We sat in silence for a time, then he said, "But this will not happen to your family because I have pardoned you."

I stared at him in disbelief. "You've pardoned me?"

"Yes," he said. "We have decided to 'let the law sleep for this night'."

I recognized the quote. "Agesilaus!" I said. Mago and I had both learned of this Spartan king from Sosylus.

"Yes, Agesilaus," he replied. "I understand why you did what you did, although I can't publicly condone it. You couldn't have told the Scipios anything of great importance; they're both dead! And I have not forgotten how you saved my life at the battle of Trebia."

"I did?" I didn't remember that at all.

"Gisco, you're just as much of a dolt as ever!" exclaimed Mago, laughing.

"I go into a trance on the battlefield and remember little of it afterward," I said. "That's how I keep my sanity. But where are Sansara and the children? You didn't put my wife in chains, did you?"

"No, of course not," said Mago. "A woman with five little children won't try to escape, and my men needed her free to control the children. Someone like you, on the other hand, who has outstanding martial skills, would naturally have to be chained." Mago grinned. "I heard that you fended off five armed men after you left Khart Hadasht."

I laughed. "You know those weren't warriors, Mago. I only had to threaten them."

"Sansara and the children are on their way to Carthage where they will be safe. They will stay in your father's household. As for you, I want you to resume your former position as my lieutenant. You will see your family when fortune permits.

"Come, let's have some wine. I'm sorry but I'm out of Falernian; the local vintage will have to do."

"Mago, this is far better than I expected, or deserved," I said, sipping my wine.

"Obviously you became far too attached to your wife, far more than Hasdrubal the Fair ever intended. But why didn't you come to me?" His expression was pained.

"I would never have reached you before the soldiers arrested me on Indibal's orders and took the child, so I went northeast where we would encounter no soldiers. Besides, you took an oath to worship and obey the gods of Carthage, Mago. Could I have asked you to break this oath and defy the gods? I was willing to defy the gods because I couldn't stand the thought of my child being burned, but I didn't feel that I could ask anyone else, especially my best friend, to endure the wrath of the gods."

"The less said about this matter the better," said Mago. "We have a lot of work to do. Now that the Romans have been soundly defeated in the field, we have to repair our alliances and deal with the tribes that deserted to the Romans. You were my right-hand man. I never found anyone who could adequately replace you, so I expect you to serve me in that capacity again."

"I owe you my life, Mago," I said. "I will do whatever you say." In the world of Carthage only Mago Barca would have had the audacity to pardon a traitor just because he was a boyhood friend. And only Mago Barca would have gotten away with it.

# THIRTEEN

## CARTHAGE LOSES SPAIN TO THE ROMANS

SANSARA
209 B.C.

Sansara," said Gisco's father. "I have a letter from Drubal. Fantastic news!"

"What is it, Aba?" I always addressed Gisco's father by their word for Papa.

"I'll read it to you," he replied.

"Beloved Aba and Uma,

"I was sorry to hear from you that Buba has died. I know she was a bit irascible at times, but she was always entertaining, with her old-fashioned notions and her stories of the old days. I still remember the time when Gisco and Mago broke the chain on her pendant and she laid into them with her cane. She was like an angry chicken! I couldn't stop laughing.

"Speaking of Gisco, Mago has pardoned him. I saw him when I went to a meeting at Mago's camp. By Melqart, that rascal gets away with everything! Always has! Buba was the only one who ever disciplined him. 'How could you pardon a traitor?' I asked Mago. 'I've crucified men for far less.' He shrugged and said 'He saved my life at Trebia, so I owed him one. Besides, I need a good quartermaster.' Such a soft-hearted fool, that Mago. If he weren't Hannibal's brother he would be a junior officer at best.

"As for the war, the Romans sent a fool named Nero to Spain, but he didn't last long. He had Hannibal's brother Hasdrubal trapped in a defile in the Black Hills, but Hasdrubal outfoxed him and got away. Unfortunately, Marcius is still there, and he's an able general. We have not been able to conquer the north. We hear from Hannibal that he is spread too thin in Italia. He has lost Capua, which allied itself to him after the battle of Cannae. He has had to retreat to Bruttium, where he has established a strong base. Aba, could you not plead his cause in the Senate? He needs more men and materiel.

"Give my love to Uma and my salutations to Sansara and her children.

"Your son, Hasdrubal."

I was thrilled that Gisco had been spared. Of course, he now owed Mago his life, and would never be released from that obligation until he or Mago died, but that was a price I was willing to pay. I began to weep with relief. Oh Gisco, my Gisco, you're alive! I hugged Aba, and we both cried tears of happiness. The children would be so happy. I couldn't wait to tell them.

"Drubal likes his brother not," I said to Aba.

Aba shook his head. "No, he never has. It grieves Uma and me but there was never anything we could do about it. Sometimes two people are so different that they never develop rapport. I am grateful that Mago pardoned Gisco. There will be those who say that what Gisco did was unforgiveable, and I understand their point of view, but, now that I've gotten to know our little Hanno, I can also understand why Gisco did it. We'll have a feast tonight and celebrate this good news!"

I wanted to ask Aba why the Carthaginians practiced child sacrifice, but I decided that the question would be rude and I probably wouldn't understand the explanation.

The children have had some ill effects from our ordeal. Giscana doesn't want to let me out of her sight, little Gisco sucks his thumb constantly, and Hanno is withdrawn and silent. He only comes out of his shell with his grandfather. They miss their little friends that they used to play with in Tarraco. But these are minor matters compared to what I feared would befall us. It helps that Megara is so calm and peaceful that I can take the children on walks accompanied by only one servant. It also helps that Gisco's parents are so kind to us. Gisco's father has arranged for the children to be tutored. I told him that Hanno was very smart and was ready to learn to read. I wish I could read and write better; then I could write letters to Gisco. With the war still going on I worry about him constantly.

I enjoy living in Carthage. It's a much richer city than Tarraco and has so many interesting things to see. Megara is beautiful and peaceful; I take the children for a walk in the gardens every day. Once a week I go shopping in the inner city, accompanied by Giscana and some of the family's servants. Gisco's father gives me an allowance to spend. He adores the children and teaches them games such as draughts and mancala. Sometimes he takes them on outings in the inner city. One time I went with them, and we went to a park where the city kept a menagerie. In one of the cages there were two huge animals that looked sort of like people except that they were covered with black hair all over their bodies, and instead of walking upright they walked bent over, and used their knuckles to support themselves when they walked. Aba said that they had been captured by Carthaginian sailors who had sailed south along the coast of Africa. The children and I could have watched them all day!

GISCO

It took some time for Mago and me to resume our old friendship. Some trust had been lost on both sides. For a long time we both avoided any reference to my sojourn among the Romans, but one evening when we were dining alone together and drinking wine, Mago brought the matter up.

"So, Gisco, how did the Romans treat you?"

"I would have to say that they treated me decently," I said. "There was never any coercion or abuse. Obviously, they had me in their power, and could have done everything they wanted to me, Sansara, and the children, but I never felt fear after I met Lucius. Lucius was Gneius Scipio's assistant, and he was the one who dealt with me."

"I think I've heard of this Lucius," said Mago. "Gorgo called him 'Gneius Scipio's puppy,' and said he was going to capture him and bring him to us so we could interrogate him. Evidently, this Lucius was a better fighter than we thought, because Gorgo never came back. One of our Celtiberian agents informed us that they had found Gorgo's body in a clearing, along with two other dead Celtiberians and three dead Romans. None of the Romans were tall, so your Lucius couldn't have been among them. The Romans had had their jugulars cut and the Celtiberians had been stabbed in their vitals with a knife or a sword. It was very strange."

"Who was Gorgo?" I asked.

"He was our double agent among the Celtiberians. He was the one who arranged their false alliance with the Romans and then their defection," said Mago. "He hated this Lucius, said something about his stepdaughter taking up with the man."

"Lucius was the only one I really got to know among the Romans," I said. "He never told me anything about his private life, though, except that he had a son in Rome. He was always kind to me and I couldn't help liking him."

"Yes," said Mago. "I suppose there are some good Romans. A pity that someday we may have to kill him. But Gisco, if you had it to do again, would you do the same thing?"

I replied without hesitation, "Yes, I would do the same thing."

Mago regarded me in silence for a time, and then said, "If you want to know the truth, it was your wife who convinced me to spare your life."

"Sansara begged you to spare my life?" I asked.

"No, she didn't beg," replied Mago, "she demanded." He laughed. "You have quite a wife. She told me that if you had allowed your son to be sacrificed, she would have killed you herself, and I have little doubt of it. But if you ever do this sort of thing again, your life won't be spared." Then he laughed again, "or maybe I'll sell you as a slave to your brother Drubal."

"I think I'd prefer the cross," I replied.

Things remained static in Spain for about a year. The Romans sent Gaius Claudius Nero to Spain with two legions. He came in pursuit of Hasdrubal Barca, and, at one point, had Hasdrubal and his army trapped in a defile. Hasdrubal pretended to negotiate with Nero, saying that he would quit Spain altogether if Nero allowed him and his army to depart, but then he dragged out the negotiations and most of his men managed to escape the trap. On a morning with thick fog, Hasdrubal and his cavalry also escaped. Nero left his army under the command of Lucius Marcius and went back to Rome.

In the meantime Hannibal continued to lose ground in Italy. The Romans, under their Consuls Quintus Fulvius Flaccus and Apius Claudius Pulcher, besieged Capua, determined to wrest it back from Hannibal. As a diversionary measure, Hannibal besieged Rome, hoping to draw the consular armies away from Capua and into a pitched battle. When this didn't work, he gave up the endeavor and returned to his base in Bruttium. The Capuans surrendered. Some of their leaders committed suicide. Those that didn't were scourged and decapitated by the Romans. The surviving population was sold into slavery.

Here in Spain, we thought that with the Scipios destroyed we were now in a fairly secure position. We did not believe that the Romans had a competent general to spare for our region. We were wrong. About two years after his father and uncle perished at our hands, young Publius Cornelius Scipio managed to get himself commissioned as Proconsul to Spain, and arrived at Tarraco with two more legions. He was twenty-five years old. Our spies in Tarraco brought word of his coming.

"Mago," I said, "do you remember the battle of Ticinus, where the Roman Consul Publius Scipio was unhorsed, wounded, and about to be killed or captured, when that crazy fool of a Roman cavalryman led a charge of his *turma* and rescued him?"

Mago grinned. "How could I forget that? It was the most audacious thing I've ever seen in my life!"

"Well, I hate to tell you this, but that crazy fool was this very Proconsul who has just arrived in Tarraco with his legions; Publius Cornelius Scipio, the son of the Scipio we slew at the Upper Baetis!"

"How do you know this, Gisco?" asked Mago.

"Because I once mentioned to Publius Scipio that I had seen him rescued at Ticinus, and he said, with great pride, that his rescuer was his son, Publius."

"Well, it's obvious that this young Scipio fears nothing," said Mago. "But people who fear nothing tend to put themselves in danger. Let us hope that he meets with some misfortune."

"That may be," I said, "but I suspect that if he has survived until now, he's learned caution. And with his father dead there will be no more need for heroics."

Had Hannibal been around to advise his two brothers and mine, I suspect that what happened next would never have taken place. The first thing the young Roman general did was to march

25,000 troops down to Khart Hadasht in seven days, and lay siege to the city. By the time any of our three armies were aware of what was going on, Scipio had taken the city. None of our generals had had the slightest inkling that Scipio would do this, and we all thought that Khart Hadasht was impregnable, so there was only a force of some 10,000 men defending the city. It turned out that there was a weak spot, the part of the city where the lagoon met the walls. At certain times the water was so shallow that men could walk through it, and it would reach only to their thighs. The walls were not so high there and could be breached with ladders. The wall was virtually undefended because the Romans appeared to be concentrated on the other side of the city, and nearly all of the defenders were there. Scipio sent a force of 500 legionaries over the wall, and they attacked our forces at the main gate and forced it open. Then Scipio's men stormed in and started killing every man in sight. The commander of the garrison agreed to surrender in order to stop the killing. Scipio thenceforth treated the inhabitants of the city with clemency.

We had lost our wealthy and beautiful Khart Hadasht, the city of my dreams. A pall of sadness settled upon our army. My only consolation was that Sansara and the children had been sent to old Carthage, so, at least for now, they were safe. Fortunately for my brother, his wife and children were staying with him in Gades. He decided to send them home to Carthage. I heard that Hannibal's wife, Imilce, had gone home to Castulo, which had returned to the Carthaginian fold after the battles of the Upper Baetis. To me, the loss of Khart Hadasht seemed to be the beginning of the end.

The conquest of Khart Hadasht greatly enriched the Romans, but that wasn't the worst of it. One of the major consequences was that all of the hostages we had held in Khart Hadasht fell into the hands of the Romans, and Scipio made the maximum use of them. He returned each of them to their respective tribes, and each of these tribes now gladly allied with the Romans. Even Indibilis and Mandonius of the Ilergites, who had been our staunch allies for years, now went over to Rome.

When spring came, Scipio, with a force of 35,000, went after the army of Hasdrubal Barca, which was at Baecula. The Romans defeated him soundly, killing 6,000 and capturing 12,000 out of a force of 25,000. Hasdrubal managed to escape. Scipio had the African prisoners sold as slaves, but freed the Spanish prisoners without ransom; another part of his scheme to endear himself to the Spaniards. He did free one of the African prisoners, however: Masiva, the young nephew of Masinissa. Perhaps he thought he might endear himself to Masinissa as well.

I went with Mago to a meeting with the two Hasdrubals. It was obvious that we needed to develop a plan of action or all of Spain would be lost.

"It is past time that I join Hannibal in Italia," Said Hasdrubal Barca. "He's been there for ten years now, and his operations are confined to Apulia and Bruttium. The Senate has not authorized supplies or reinforcements to him in years. I will raise an army among the tribes of Spain that are still loyal to us, and take it over the Alps. I'll get there earlier in the year than Hannibal did, and, from what I've heard, the natives will not be as hostile to us as they were to Hannibal. We should have an easier time and lose far fewer men. It will be up to you, Mago, and you, Hasdrubal, son of Gisco, to keep Spain in Carthaginian hands."

Mago replied, "I'm not sure how much we can trust the Spanish tribesmen at this point. I think we need to look elsewhere to find troops who will help us defend our interests in Spain. I'm going to go to the Balearic Islands and recruit there. I'll leave my men with Hasdrubal, son of Gisco. I don't think that we should engage with the Romans until I return with the Balearics. We can have Masinissa and his Numidians harass the Romans and their allies in the meantime."

After the meeting I asked my brother if he had heard anything from our father. "He has written me, and everyone is well except Buba. She passed away last winter. Your wife and children are there and they have arranged to have the children tutored." He shook his head and sighed. "Gisco, you should thank Melqart that your commanding officer was Mago and not me. I would have had you crucified, brother or not!"

"Yes, I know," I replied. "You're right. I'll sacrifice a lamb to Melqart."

"On the other hand, I wouldn't have had you abducted from Tarraco," said my brother, "because if I crucified you it would have grieved Aba and Uma."

"Is Aba angry with me?" I asked.

"He was," replied my brother. "But it seems your little Hanno has wormed his way into his grandfather's heart. A charmer, that one. Now Aba thinks you did the right thing. Of course, you always were his favorite." I did not deny the assertion. I suspected that there was some truth in it. I had long since learned that there was no point in arguing with my jealous sibling.

I went with Mago to the Balearics. On the way there, we stopped at Carthage and I was able to spend a few days with Sansara and the children. I had not seen them in over two years, and it was startling to see how much they had grown. Giscana was now twelve and very pretty. It would soon be time to find a husband for her. Gisco was now nine, Hanno six, Himilco four and Elissa two. All the children looked strong and healthy and they all seemed intelligent. My parents had made sure that the older three were being properly tutored in Phoenician and Greek.

"Aba," said my son Gisco, "Can you take us fishing?" He had fond memories of our outings with Demetrios.

"I won't be in Carthage for very long," I said, "but I'll see what I can do."

"Why were you gone so long?" asked my son. "Why do you have to go away so soon? We missed you!"

"Well, son, there's a war, and when there's a war a man has to go off and fight in it," I said, "if not, we could be conquered by the enemy and killed or sold into slavery."

"Will there always be a war?" asked my son.

"I don't know," I said, "the last one lasted twenty-three years and this one has already gone on for nine. I hope it ends before you have to fight in it."

Little Gisco looked troubled. "Do you think Carthage will win?" he asked.

"I hope so," I replied. "I think it will depend on whether Hannibal's brother Hasdrubal can join him in Italia."

I made inquiries and paid a fisherman to take me and little Gisco and Hanno out on his boat. It was a lovely day and we each caught several fish. Gisco could net them on his own, but we had to help little Hanno.

## MAGO

While we were in Carthage, I gave a report to the Senate.

"Elders of Carthage," I said, "I will not lie to you. We are having difficulties in Spain. The Roman general Scipio, son of the Scipio whom we slew at the Upper Baetis, has come to avenge his father and uncle. He has taken the port of Khart Hadasht, and he has defeated our forces under Hasdrubal Barca at Baecula. If we want to hold onto Spain and the silver mines that bring such riches to Carthage, we must have more men and supplies. I will be going to the Balearic Islands to recruit soldiers. Hasdrubal Barca is planning to take his army over the Alps and join Hannibal in Italia. Together they will defeat the Romans once and for all. But if we want to hold onto Spain against the forces of Scipio, Carthage must send another army to replace the one Hasdrubal Barca is taking with him. Elders of Carthage, can we depend on your support for our efforts in Spain?"

I looked out at the rows of Senators. The reaction was subdued, and the Senators looked anxious. I could see that there was little enthusiasm for the war effort. Sitting in the front row was Hanno, my father's old enemy. A frown on his face, he clutched his cane in his withered right hand.

Hanno the Great stood up to speak. "Mago, son of Hamilcar, this war has been going on for ten years now, and we are no closer to victory than we were the last time you spoke to this assemblage. In fact, at that time we were in a good position to make peace, and now we are much at a disadvantage. We have lost Khart Hadasht, Capua, Tarentum, and Syracuse. Did I not tell this assembly that we should have made peace with the Romans after Cannae? Did I not, in fact, tell this assembly ten years ago that we should not go to war with the Romans? Who listens to old Hanno? You have dug a hole, Mago, you and your brothers Hannibal and Hasdrubal. You and all of Carthage will be buried in it before you are done."

Senator Himilco, who had always supported the goals of our family, got up and spoke.

"Senator Hanno tells us 'I told you so,' in his usual fashion. But what would Rab Hanno have us do? Surrender? Leave the silver mines to the Romans? Rab Hanno is not the only one here who can say 'I told you so.' In ten years Carthage has sent virtually nothing and no one to the aid of Hannibal. Is it any wonder that he was unable to defend Capua? Men die in war, and they must be replaced. If not, your army becomes too weak to fight, even if led by such a brilliant general as Hannibal. I say we give Mago everything he is asking for, and may it come to pass that Hasdrubal Barca unites his forces with Hannibal and destroys our enemy once and for all."

In the end the Senate agreed to send another general to Spain with an army, and agreed that I should recruit among the Balearics. They gave the go-ahead to my brother's plan to cross the Alps and unite with Hannibal. Hasdrubal had not waited for their permission. He gathered up an army from the tribes still loyal to Carthage and crossed the Pyrenees, hoping to recruit from the Gauls of Gallia and the Gauls and other non-Roman peoples of northern Italia.

## GISCO

Mago and I returned from the Balearics with 5,000 foot soldiers, and joined up with the new general whose name was Hanno. My brother Drubal had also recruited a number of soldiers from among the Celtiberians. Unfortunately, we were attacked by the Romans, under Scipio's lieutenant Marcus Junius Silanus, and the Celtiberians were routed from their camp. Hanno and many of his men were captured, and Mago and his soldiers driven off. We retreated to Gades. To make things worse, the authorities in Gades refused to open their gates to us. Mago besieged the city, and when they surrendered, he had the officials publicly crucified. Despite the fact that the citizens of Gades were mostly of Phoenician descent, they were sullen and coldly polite. Mago found it necessary to rule them with an iron fist. Perhaps they suspected that, with the loss of Khart Hadasht, the days of Carthaginian rule in Spain were numbered, and they could not rely on us to protect them from the Romans.

Mago had made his headquarters in the Governor's palace, in the quarters of a man he had crucified. As his lieutenant, I was also assigned quarters in the palace. We still had some 30,000 troops who were camped outside of the city. I knew that with the beginning of spring there would be another mobilization, and I was already organizing the logistics involved: supplies of food, armor, weapons, and horses; mercenary pay, and the training of troops. Young Scipio had already proven himself an able general, and I was not looking forward to facing him, once again, in battle.

Mago summoned me to his headquarters. The previous occupants, whose remains were still moldering on crosses outside the gates of the city, had been surrounded by elegance. There were ornate wall hangings depicting scenes from the epic Gilgamesh, and fine statues in both Phoenician and Greek style. Mago's desk was elaborately wrought of ebony, and highly polished.

I immediately knew from the expression on Mago's face that something was seriously wrong. His complexion was gray, his eyes bloodshot, his mouth set in a deep frown. He was poring over a parchment. He did not greet me or offer me wine. I had never seen Mago so downcast.

"This is from Hannibal," he said, "written months ago. It just arrived last night."

"It's bad news?"

He handed me the letter.

My dear Mago,

I hope this reaches you and finds you well. I am afraid I bear distressing news. Our brother, Hasdrubal, is dead, his mission a complete failure. He did, indeed, make it over the Alps with a goodly army, and recruited some troops from the Gauls. Unfortunately, the messengers he sent to contact me lost their way and were intercepted by Roman soldiers. Their messages were translated and given to Claudius Nero, the Roman Consul here in Apulia. Nero marched a contingent of 7,000 veteran soldiers to reinforce the other Consul, Marcus Livius, and their combined forces annihilated Hasdrubal's army. I learned of this when my men brought me our brother's severed head, which Nero's men had flung into our camp. As you might imagine, the sight sickened me, and I have not recovered my spirits.

The rest of the news is not favorable either. The Romans won't fight me head on in a pitched battle. Their strategy is to make war on our allies and deprive me of their assistance. They have punished our allies ruthlessly, destroying the populations of both Capua and Tarentum. Gradually they have reconquered most of the territory that came into our alliance after Cannae, and now our forces are confined to Bruttium.

Mago, if you and Hasdrubal, son of Gisco, can regain control of Spain by defeating Scipio, you must raise an army and bring me reinforcements. Together we can go back on the offensive. If we are to salvage this situation, I will need your help. If I had known how little help I would receive from Carthage, I would have stayed in Spain and let the Romans come to us. As it is, we stand to lose both Spain and Italia, and the Senators who have denied me reinforcements may repent of it when they see Roman standards at their walls!

Always,

Hannibal

"By all the gods!" I exclaimed. "They severed his head! How barbaric! Hannibal always treated dead Roman generals with the utmost respect!"

"Claudius Nero had better hope he never falls into my hands!" growled Mago.

"What are we going to do now, Mago?"

"We will go ahead with our plan to defeat Scipio," he said. "I still have 30,000 men and your brother has about 25,000, as well. Combined, we outnumber Scipio significantly. If I survive this battle, win or lose, I'm going to arrange to bring reinforcements to Hannibal in Italia."

"Will we be crossing the Alps again?" I asked. I was not at all keen on doing that!

"No," said Mago. "Carthage was once a great maritime power. It's time Carthage revived its fleet. I will campaign for a fleet to be built, and we will invade Italia by ship."

I knew that when Mago made up his mind to do something, only his death would stop him from doing it.

Mago and my brother combined forces to make one more effort to defeat Scipio. We had some 55,000 troops, as compared to some 45,000 on Scipio's side. Our two armies camped near each other in the vicinity of Ilipa. Mago sent Masinissa and his Numidian horsemen to attack Scipio's cavalry, but Scipio had set up an ambush, and Masinissa was driven off with heavy losses. For several days Scipio brought out his forces in battle array late in the morning, but then declined combat. Then, one day he brought them out very early in the morning. My brother Drubal hastily assembled our forces and put them into formation. I remembered what Lucius had said about the Romans learning from Hannibal. Scipio was doing what Hannibal had done at Trebia, goading the enemy's forces into battle before they had a chance to eat. The battle reminded me of Cannae, only this time we were on the losing side! The Romans wiped out our forces except for about 6,000 who took refuge on a mountain, and even these soon surrendered. Mago, Drubal, and I managed to escape and make our way by ship to Carthage. All of Spain was now in the hands of Scipio.

SANSARA
206 B.C.

"Gisco! You're home! I love you! I love you!" I flew to Gisco's embrace. He smiled and we hugged for a long time. Our lips met and did not want to part.

"Is the war over now?" I asked. "Are you back for good?"

Gisco sighed. "Spain is lost, but no, the war is not over; not while Hannibal remains in Italia. I'm sorry, my little dove, but Mago intends to invade Italia by ship and I must go with him. But for now I'm home. It will take couple of years to build the ships we need and to recruit enough men."

Aba's house is crowded. Not only did Gisco come back but Drubal had sent his wife Amashtar and their two children Caphonbal and Bomilcar home, and they occupied part of the mansion. Drubal returned home shortly after Gisco did, but he spends most of his time at the Senate. He has been appointed a member of the committee of 104, which oversees the affairs of Carthage. Gisco takes no part in politics; he prefers to help his father with his business.

Amashtar is one of those Carthaginian women who look down upon the Spanish wives of highborn Carthaginians as provincials and simpletons. She is condescending to me and addresses me in a loud voice as though she thinks that that will improve my comprehension of her Phoenician. Actually I understand her Phoenician perfectly well. She is a devoted mother, but both of her children are somewhat spoiled. Bomilcar is a nice boy, but childish. He and my son Gisco are on about the same level of maturity, so they get along. Caphonbal is seventeen and quite the beauty. Her father spoils her even more than her mother does, letting her buy whatever she wants from the marketplace. I fear she may have a bad influence on Giscana. Giscana practically worships her cousin. Caphonbal has taught Giscana how to dance and use makeup, and gives her pointers on how to flirt with boys. Caphonbal has many suitors and, at fourteen, Giscana is starting to attract male attention as well. I have warned Giscana not to let any man be alone with her. Gisco wants to make a good marriage for her, and that won't happen if she lets a man debauch her.

Mago now lives at his deceased father's mansion in Megara, not far from us. Only he and his sister Saponibal, the widow of Hasdrubal the Fair, and a few servants, live there now.

One day Gisco said, "Sansara, Aba is giving a party tomorrow night. We are inviting Mago and Saponibal, Himilco and his wife, and various other Barca supporters from Megara. There will be a big surprise for you."

"A surprise? What kind of surprise?" I asked.

"I'm not allowed to tell you," he grinned, "but I think it will make you very happy."

I spent the next day wondering what the surprise might be. That evening Aba and Uma spread a magnificent table with platters of lamb, mullet, duck, and sweetmeats, all kinds of vegetables, olives, fine wines, fresh fruits, and several kinds of desserts. Extra couches were brought out to accommodate the guests. Gisco asked me to greet the guests as they arrived.

Mago and Saponibal were among the last to arrive, and they were accompanied by none other than Imilce! We dove into each other's arms and hugged and cried. I forgot everything else and took Imilce away with me to our apartment.

"Imilce! I thought I'd never see you again!"

"Oh, Sansara, I can't tell you how glad I am to be here! It was so frightening! I was in Castulo, and Scipio's men laid siege to the city. We really weren't prepared for a siege, and we soon ran out of food and were collecting rainwater to drink. Scipio was besieging Iliturgis at the same time, and when he finally broke down their walls he killed every man, woman, and child in the city! A witness to the massacre sneaked into Castulo and brought word to my father, who decided to surrender the city. Father was afraid that if the Romans knew that I was there, they would take me to Rome as a prisoner, so he arranged to have me sneak out of the city and escape. He gave me enough gold that I was able to bribe a merchant to bring me to Carthage."

"What happened to the people of Castulo after they surrendered?" I asked.

"Before I left Spain I got a message from my father saying that Scipio had installed a garrison there, but had allowed the residents to stay," said Imilce. "Now the Romans rule all of Spain, and I will never be able to go back."

I filled Imilce in on all the things that had happened to me since we last saw each other; then I remembered that I was hungry and she must be too. "Imilce, this has been such a wonderful surprise, but you must be starving. Let's get some food."

I am thrilled to have my husband home and my best friend nearby after all of these lonely months. The only thing that disturbs my tranquility is the knowledge that in a year or two Gisco will be going back to Italia with Mago, back to war and the fields of carnage. Mago follows Hannibal blindly, and Gisco follows Mago blindly. Hannibal. How I loathe that man! Everyone around me worships him, but to me he is a monster. I hold my tongue around his devotees. If only Hasdrubal the Fair had not been assassinated. He seemed to be a reasonable man; he might have kept Hannibal in check.

What is it about men that they devote their lives to war and revenge? Are the Romans monsters? Those I met in Tarraco seemed no more monstrous than anyone else. Imilce says that they killed every man, woman, and child in Iliturgis, but is it not war that makes men into monsters?

# FOURTEEN

## MAGO AND GISCO RETURN TO ITALIA

GISCO
205 B.C.

Mago was a man obsessed. Determined to raise a new army and join Hannibal, he constantly lobbied and pestered an increasingly reluctant Senate. It took nearly two years before he was able to gather enough ships and men to make his own expedition to Italia. There were no safe harbors in southern Italia, so Mago decided that the best thing to do would be to take his ships to the land of the Inguanian Gauls on the Ligurian coast. The Inguanians had a long history of hostility to Rome, and Mago believed that he could recruit enough of them to provide a substantial manpower boost for Hannibal. When all was in readiness Mago paid me a visit at my father's mansion in

Megara. Aba and Uma greeted him politely and directed servants to bring us fruit, bread, and wine, and then withdrew so that we could talk privately.

"This wine is good, Gisco. Where did you get it?"

"I persuaded Aba to plant grapes on our estate near Nepheris. This is from our first crop. It will be even better when it has had a chance to age."

Mago looked pensive. He sighed and then set down his cup. "I think that being a merchant suits you more than being a soldier, Gisco, but I will be needing your services for this campaign. We sail in three days. Are you with me?"

"Of course, Mago. You know I would deny you nothing, Mago, not even my life."

"Perhaps I did a good thing in sparing you from the cross, Gisco. I've always wondered," he laughed.

"Sometimes mercy pays off," I said. "Remember when Scipio sent Masinissa's nephew Masiva back to him unharmed? Now he has Masinissa eating out of his hand."

"Don't remind me!" said Mago. "At least we have Syphax back in the fold, thanks to your brother and his daughter Caphonbal. She'll see to it that he fights for Carthage if it comes to that." My brother had married his daughter off to the Numidian king.

"I take it that my brother has no interest in this venture?"

"I think it is better that Drubal stay here and promote the interests of our party," said Mago. "To tell you the truth, I was never comfortable working with him in Spain. An army with two generals is like a horse with two heads. The second head just gets in the way."

I laughed. "Better for me too," I said. "Drubal and I get along best at a distance."

I had enjoyed being with my wife and children for these two years, and Sansara had given me another son, whom we named Gillimas. Sansara was nursing the babe when I came to our bedchamber.

"Mago is taking you with him," she said.

"Yes, Sansara, I must go."

"I know, Gisco. Any other choice would be dishonorable after he spared your life. Isn't it strange? That's exactly what I told Mago, that it would be dishonorable to take your life after you had saved his. That is why he spared your life. Now perhaps both of you will die. Will there never be an end to this accursed war?"

"I don't know, Sansara. I hope so."

She put the baby in his cradle and put her arms around me. The urge to become one flesh overtook us and, for a time, we were so absorbed in our pleasure that we entirely forgot about the cruelties of this world.

We sailed to the Ligurian coast with 30 ships and 5,000 men recruited from the Libyans, the Numidians, and the Balearics. The Inguanians welcomed us and we established a camp there. The city of Zena surrendered to us without a fight, so we had a seaport and a base. Unfortunately, there was no way for us to join Hannibal. All routes southward were securely blocked by the Romans.

In the meantime, Scipio had finished his work in Spain, dealing with cities and tribes that had not cooperated with the Romans, and in a few cases, destroying whole towns. He returned to Rome and was elected Consul. He proclaimed to the Roman Senate that he planned to invade Africa and carry the war to the gates of Carthage. It took him a year to recruit, train, and prepare his troops, but at last he invaded Africa with a force of some 16,000 foot soldiers and 1,600 cavalry. It seemed that Masinissa had defected to Scipio even before he left Spain. He was back in Africa and would join forces with Scipio.

During that time, my brother had not been idle. His idea to marry his daughter Caphonbal to Syphax, the king of the Maseasyli, was nothing short of brilliant. Syphax had signed a treaty with Scipio, but now he had been lured back to our side. My niece, Caphonbal, was now a stunningly beautiful young woman of twenty-one who could charm the loincloth off of most any man. Caphonbal had been much attracted to Masinissa, but now Masinissa was the enemy, and Caphonbal knew her duty. She was a loyal and obedient daughter. Her instructions were to make sure that Syphax fought for Carthage. My brother and Syphax gathered up a combined army of 80,000 infantry and 13,000 cavalry.

Scipio tried to persuade Syphax to renounce his allegiance to Carthage, but Syphax was hopelessly enamored of Caphonbal. One night Scipio sent his forces to both Syphax's camp and my brother's, and set fire to both camps. The soldier's huts were made of dry straw and were highly flammable. Out of combined forces of my brother and Syphax only some 35,000 escaped. The rest were killed or captured. Both my brother Drubal and Syphax managed to escape. Drubal fled back to Carthage, and Syphax removed his camp to a fortified place about eight miles away.

Drubal recruited all the men he could from Carthage, but these were inexperienced soldiers. He also managed to import some 4,000 Celtiberian mercenaries from Spain. He joined forces with the remains of Syphax's troops, and they gave Scipio battle on the Great Plains. Once again it was a disaster for Carthage. Syphax went back to Cirta and tried to raise and train a new army, but Scipio sent his lieutenant Gaius Laelius, along with Masinissa, to pursue him. Syphax's untrained army was no match for the forces of Laelius and Masinissa. Syphax was thrown from his horse and captured alive. I don't know exactly what happened concerning my niece, Caphonbal. Rumor had it that she seduced Masinissa into marrying her. When Scipio forbade the union, she took poison to prevent herself from being taken prisoner by the Romans. One story is that Masinissa provided her with it.

Carthage sued for peace, and Scipio granted a truce. But the Carthaginian Senate sent messengers by ship to both Bruttium and the Ligurian coast to order both Hannibal and Mago to return to Carthage to defend the city.

Around this time, the Romans decided it was time to rid Italia of Mago, so they sent Publius Quinctilius Varus, a Praetor, and Marcus Cornelius, a Proconsul, with a legion each, to engage us in battle. I fought by Mago's side in hand-to-hand combat with the Romans. Our forces were holding their own, but we were starting to show signs of fatigue. Suddenly I heard a loud cry.

"Aaah! Gisco! Help me!" I turned toward the voice. It was Mago. He had been struck in the thigh by a javelin, a wound similar to the one Hannibal had sustained at the siege of Saguntum.

"Mago!" I cried. "What do we do now?"

"We withdraw, Gisco. Get a stretcher. Have the soldiers cover our retreat and get me down to the port. I will need a surgeon."

We made a stretcher and transferred Mago to it; then we began an orderly retreat, with the rear guard continuing to engage the Romans. When darkness fell, the Romans returned to their camp, and we made our way down to Zena. It took two days to get there, and by then Mago was burning with fever. Unfortunately there was no time to take him to a surgeon because the Romans were besieging the city and we had to get all of our soldiers aboard ships before the Romans broke through.

It was clear that the wound was badly infected, and that if the leg were not amputated, Mago would die; but there was no surgeon, nor even a butcher, among the crew. I stayed by Mago's side. "Gisco, when you see Hannibal, tell him that his brother, Mago, was loyal to him to the end. Tell him I will see him in the nether world. Tell him I died for Carthage." Then he said, "I love you, Gisco; you were always my best friend."

I had no idea whether I would see Hannibal again, but I assured Mago I would relate everything he had said. I did not bother to reassure Mago that he wasn't going to die, because we both knew that he was dying. Both of us had seen enough death in this war to know when it was coming.

MAGO

I am dying. That much is certain. My wound throbs, my thigh is hot and swollen. I try to control the chattering of my teeth. My breathing is ragged and labored. The worst of it is that I cannot get my muscles to relax; I cannot get comfortable and sleep.

We are on a Carthaginian ship bound for Africa. Gisco sits by my side, looking lost and helpless. He wipes my forehead with a damp rag. That's all he knows to do. I have given him my last instructions.

What is it that the Romans say? *Dulce et decorum est pro patria mori.* That is little comfort. I have failed. I failed to keep Spain in Carthaginian hands. I failed to join with Hannibal in Italy. I failed to save Carthage from the Romans. Sixteen years of war and I will not live to see the end of it.

Ah, the light fades.

## GISCO

Three days out to sea, Mago passed away. I felt as if a part of me had been amputated. I have no words to describe my desolation. The captain of the vessel perceived my distress and awkwardly tried to comfort me. He put his hand on my shoulder. "Mago Barca," he said, "he was a man's man." He had been far more than that to me.

"We are bound for Adrudentum, the same place where Hannibal will land," said the captain. "We will deliver Mago's body to Hannibal." I nodded, unable to speak.

I slept during most of the passage, eating and drinking very little. The crew did their best to preserve Mago's body, keeping it soaked with salt water. Finally we landed in Adrudentum, and I was sent to Hannibal's camp to deliver the bad news. I thought that perhaps Hannibal would kill the messenger, but at this point I really didn't care.

SANSARA

"No, my lady," said Nambal, Aba's steward, "you cannot go shopping in the inner city today. It's not safe. The mob is rioting."

"What's going on?" I asked.

"They're desperate for food," he replied. "The Romans have been ravaging the countryside and destroying all the crops, so food prices have soared. Poor families can no longer afford to eat. Last week nearly a whole fleet of Roman ships was caught in a storm and blown to our shores. The people ran the crews off and plundered the cargos. Now the Romans say we have broken the truce and we are once more at war.

"It is still safe to walk about in Megara," he added. "The merchants have hired extra armed guards in case any of the rabble try to enter."

Things were getting more and more uncomfortable in Carthage, and the war was coming ever closer. Carthage had been spared the depredations of war all these years that Hannibal was on the offensive, but now it was time for the Romans to wreak their revenge. I wished that the children and I were somewhere else, anywhere else.

Aba received word that Hannibal had landed and had established a base at Adrudentum, some six days' march from Carthage. Chaos still reigned in the city, however, and toward evening a man came to the mansion. Nambal admitted him, and he prostrated himself before Gisco's Aba.

We were in the common room and I was watching Aba play a game of mancala with young Gisco. Aba summoned the messenger to rise.

"I bring bad tidings, Rab Gisco," he said. "I am sorry."

"Tell me, young man," replied Aba. "Do not be afraid."

"Your son, Hasdrubal, is dead. He fell on his sword. The mob was demanding his crucifixion, blaming him for Carthage's defeat."

Aba turned pale, tried to rise, and then slumped back in his chair. Minutes passed in silence, then Aba said, "Go with Ba-al, young man. Please have them bring the body to us so that we can prepare for the cremation. Nambal, please pay this young man and show him out."

We sat in silence. Even young Gisco realized that there was nothing to say. Finally I put my arm around Aba and whispered "I'm so sorry, Aba."

Tears were running down Aba's cheeks, and he could only nod in response. Finally, he said, "Nambal, bring everyone in the household here. We may as well get this over with."

When we were all assembled, Aba pronounced the evil tidings. "We are now in mourning for our Hasdrubal, who, this day, has taken his own life. You all know the mourning practices: somber clothes, no celebrations. We decline all social invitations. We sacrifice five times to Ba-al—two lambs, two goats, and an ox."

Uma and Amashtar were weeping. Caphonbal was no longer among us. We had not yet learned her fate but assumed that she was still in Cirta. My children were solemn but did not cry. They had not been close to their Uncle Drubal. Bomilcar announced, "Grandfather, I am going tomorrow with some of my friends to join Hannibal. Father had me trained in the arts of war, and Hannibal will need every fighter he can get."

"No!" Amashtar shrieked. "Bomilcar, you will not go! I have just lost my husband. I can't bear it. You must not leave me!"

"Uma," replied Bomilcar calmly, "this is my duty. I'm nineteen and have been trained as a soldier. It was Caphonbal's duty to marry old Syphax, and it is my duty to fight for Carthage and defend her gates from the Romans. How could you expect me to shirk such a duty?"

"Amashtar, the boy is right," said Aba. "You cannot have him dishonor the family by being a coward and refusing to fight for his country." Amashtar rose and fled in tears. I was glad that young Gisco and Hanno were not of age to fight.

# FIFTEEN

## AT THE MERCY OF ROME

GISCO

Hannibal came out of his tent to meet me. "Gisco," he said, "where is Mago?"

I fell to my knees and wept. Hannibal knew what I had to say without my having to say it.

"He's gone, isn't he?" asked Hannibal. I nodded. He turned to Maharbal. "Take Gisco to a tent, give him food and wine. I'll talk to him later."

"No, wait, Hannibal," I said, "we have his body. It's still on the ship. He should be cremated soon."

"Thank you, Gisco," he said. "We'll see to it. You eat and get some rest."

The next day Hannibal came to see me. He had aged tremendously since I had seen him last. It had been fourteen years. He had been about thirty and in the prime of his manhood. Now he was forty-four, his hair graying at the temples and his face deeply lined, now etched with grief. I related to him what Mago had asked me to tell him. Hannibal nodded. Then he smiled.

Harking back to the jest he made on the morning of the battle of Cannae, he said, "I understand that the Romans actually did have a Gisco among them for a time." Seeing my look of chagrin, he said, "Don't worry, Gisco. I won't punish you. If Mago thought you deserved punishment he would have done it. I'm not going to overrule his judgment.

"Mago loved you, you know," he continued.

"Yes, I know," I replied.

"But do you know why he loved you?" he asked. I shook my head.

Hannibal laughed. "When we were children, Hasdrubal and I were always telling Mago what to do. You were the only one he could boss around. He wanted desperately to be superior to someone and you were it." I smiled, realizing that there was some truth to what Hannibal was saying. "But he loved you for another reason as well," he continued, "you are a person with no guile. Perhaps the only such person he ever met. People like you are rare, especially among Carthaginians."

"I don't think that is quite true," I said, "I've been known to lie if circumstances demand it."

"Yes, I suppose you are capable of lying if circumstances compel it," he said, "but it doesn't come naturally to you, as it does to most men. Mago once said to me, 'if you ever want to know the truth, just ask Gisco. He won't just tell you what he thinks you want to hear, as so many men do'.

"So tell me, how is your Latin?" he asked.

"Passable," I said. "I had a tutor for four years."

"I'm planning to ask Scipio for a meeting," he said. "Perhaps we can come to an agreement. I am not confident that we can win this coming battle, and it might be best to try to avoid it."

"Why don't you think we'll win?" I asked.

"I get the sense that this Scipio is not your ordinary Roman general," he said. "I think his military talents are similar to mine. He is superior in cavalry, and his men are all well trained. My veterans are well trained, but my front lines are not. I have elephants, but my elephants could become more of a liability than an asset if the Romans are smart. Elephants are more of a psychological than a tactical weapon, and it's not wise to depend on them too much. I have reason to believe that Scipio has studied my tactics and learned from them. I will do the best I can with what I have, but I fear our Carthage may be doomed."

I thought of the words of Indibal, that my sacrifice would save Carthage. "Do you think, Hannibal, that if I had allowed my son to be sacrificed, the war would have turned out differently?" Hannibal looked at me as though I had lost my mind.

"Let me tell you something, Gisco," he said, "if I had known sixteen years ago what I know now, I would never have taken on this war against the Romans. I completely misunderstood and underestimated them. Our efforts were doomed from the start. The Romans are unlike any other people. Any other nation would have sued for peace after Cannae. The Romans cannot be conquered. If you can't annihilate them, they will defeat you in the end. The only thing you would have accomplished in sacrificing your son would have been to blight your life and the life of your wife. Every time you looked at the face of a little child after that, you would have felt agony. It would have destroyed you, little by little, and done nothing for Carthage. The Romans find strength in their gods, but our Carthaginian religion is part of our weakness."

My nephew Bomilcar, now nineteen, rode out to our camp at Adrudentum. He bore ill tidings for Hannibal and for me. There had been civil strife on the streets of Carthage, and my brother, fearing the violence of the mob, had taken his own life. Drubal had not loved me the way Mago had, but I mourned for him. I felt the need to go to Carthage and comfort my parents, but I knew that my duty lay here with Hannibal.

We moved our camp to Zama, some five days' march from Carthage. Not far from us lay the camps of the Romans and of Masinissa's Numidians. Hannibal sent a messenger with a flag of truce to request a meeting with Scipio. Scipio consented, and we arranged a time and a place.

I went with Hannibal to the meeting place. The land around us was arid and desolate. If we could not come to an agreement it would soon be a battlefield. We set up a makeshift table and cushions, and sat down. Then Scipio arrived, accompanied by none other than my old friend Lucius! My jaw dropped open and so did his, but neither of us thought it safe to acknowledge the other, so after a moment Lucius just nodded to me and sat down beside Scipio.

Scipio turned to Lucius and asked, "Is something wrong, Lucius?"

"No, Publius," he said. "It must be that I'm just a bit over-whelmed at seeing Hannibal in the flesh for the first time." I was surprised that Lucius was on a first-name basis with his superior, just as I was with Hannibal.

"We meet at last, Proconsul Scipio." said Hannibal. "How ironic it is that I first fought the Romans in a pitched battle, sixteen years ago, against your father, and now, fortune decrees that I sup-plicate for peace with his son. In this the gods have a disposition to sport with events."

"Yes, Hannibal," said Scipio. "This war has gone on for many years. Both my father and my uncle, and many others have perished." Both men spoke in Greek, and no translation was necessary.

"And I have lost both of my brothers, Hasdrubal and Mago, men of consummate bravery and ability," said Hannibal. "Perhaps it would have been better if we Carthaginians had been content with our empire in Africa and you Romans with yours in Italia, but events are more easily censured than retrieved."

"In both of these wars that your country and mine have fought," said Scipio, "you, yourselves, were the aggressors. In the first war it was the danger that threatened our allies, the Mamertines, and in this war the destruction of Saguntum that girded us with just and pious arms. The gods are witnesses who determined the issue of the former war and will determine the issue of this present war according to right and justice."

Hannibal sighed. I could see he regarded Scipio as a fanatic. "Be that as it may, you would do well to arrange a peace with us here and now. I suspect that your mind may be more disposed to conquest than to peace, but you should consider not only those things that have happened, but also those that may yet occur. You can't depend on Fortuna; she's a fickle goddess. You could lose everything you've gained over the course of years in a single hour. In nothing less than in war do events correspond to men's calculation. Everything is at your disposal when adjusting a peace, but in battle you must be content with the fortune the gods shall impose. What I was at Trasimene, Scipio, you are today. Rarely does a man consider the uncertainty of events whom fortune has never deceived."

"I am well aware of the instability of human affairs," said Scipio. "I consider the influence of fortune and know very well that all of our measures are liable to a thousand casualties. If you had come to me to solicit peace before I set out for Africa, my conduct would have savored of arrogance and oppression if I rejected you, but now, when I have dragged you into Africa by manual force despite your resistance and evasion, I am not obligated to treat you with respect. You have offered us nothing that we have not already gained by our victories in this war. Indeed we must insist upon a compensation for the ships of Sextus Octavius, together with their stores, that Carthage seized and plundered during a time of truce, when they were washed upon your shores by a storm. If you agree to such terms then I may have matter to lay before my counsel, but if these things appear oppressive, prepare for war, since you could not brook the terms of peace."[9]

Hannibal did not agree to the terms, and we returned to our camp to prepare for the coming battle. Personally, I think that Scipio had his heart set on defeating Hannibal on the field of battle. It had been his consuming ambition for the past sixteen years, and he wasn't about to deny himself this opportunity for glory. He couldn't actually say this because he might be accused of sacrificing Roman lives needlessly.

"Gisco, you will be in the third line among the veterans, second in command to Bostar," said Hannibal. "I recall that you are good with a sword."

The day of the battle, we assembled in three lines. The least experienced troops, volunteers from Carthage and surrounding villages, in front; survivors who had fought under my brother and Mago behind them; and Hannibal's veterans who had come over from Italia in the rear. In front of our ranks Hannibal assembled his elephants. Our Spanish cavalry occupied one flank, and our Numidian cavalry the other. I was fully armored and led the left wing of the veterans.

Hannibal unleashed the eighty elephants, and they charged toward the Roman lines. The Roman cavalrymen blew their *bucina* and *cornua* loudly to disconcert the elephants, and some of them charged back toward our lines, creating disorder in the ranks. Others continued to charge forward, but the Romans somehow cleared a path for them, and they passed through the ranks without doing significant harm.

Our front lines engaged with theirs, and our cavalry on each wing engaged with the corresponding Roman cavalry. The left wing of the Roman cavalry was led our former ally, Masinissa, and the right wing by Scipio's lieutenant Gaius Laelius.

---

[9]  Ibid Book XXX.30.31

After a time, both of the middle ranks in each army were engaged. It was clear that Scipio's younger, less experienced troops were still far better than our poorly trained volunteers. Still, it was early afternoon before Hannibal called his veterans to join the fighting. We fought hand to hand with Scipio's veterans for some time, neither side giving way. I slew a number of Romans with my sword. But around mid-afternoon, we were attacked on both flanks by Scipio's cavalry. Not even the most experienced of foot soldiers can stand up to cavalry. I was successful for a while at dodging their swords, but I was getting exhausted, and knew that my energy couldn't last. A Roman cavalryman came at me brandishing his sword.

"Drop your sword, Gisco," he shouted. "I don't want to kill you."

"Lucius!" I croaked.

"It's over, Gisco," he said. "Carthage is defeated. Drop your sword. Don't die just to prove your bravery."

I dropped my sword. Lucius directed two of his men to escort me off the field. I heard him tell them in Latin, "He's a highborn Carthaginian. He may have some ransom value."

I was taken to the part of the camp where they kept prisoners, and put in chains. With so many prisoners, our food and water were tightly rationed. I, who had accompanied Hannibal across the Alps and through the swamps, was no stranger to hardship, but other than the time I was kidnapped by Mago's agents, nothing in my experience compared with being a prisoner in chains. I soon wished that I had died on the battlefield. The prospect of being sold into slavery weighed on my mind. What would become of Carthage, of Sansara and the children, of Aba and Uma? Sixteen years of war, all this slaughter and depredation on both sides, all for naught.

I was luckier than most. I only had minor wounds and bruises. Other prisoners had more serious wounds. Some were moaning in pain. On my right a boy was lying prostrate, mumbling in delirium.

He looked just a year or two older than my son Gisco. On my left was a man in his early thirties, dressed in a bedraggled tunic. I must have been a sorry sight because he said, "Uncle, aren't you a bit old to have been out here on the battlefield fighting?"

"What?" I said, "I'm only forty."

"Ah, I thought you were about fifty," he replied. "One of Hannibal's veterans?"

"Yes," I said. "I went over the Alps with him."

"Ah, no wonder you look so old!" He exclaimed. "What do you think the Romans will do to us?"

"The Romans usually sell prisoners of war into slavery," I said. "They may crucify me because I was an officer, but I don't think you have to worry about that."

"My master promised me freedom if I went to fight in place of his son, but it looks as though I will just go from one slavery to another," said the man. "Are the Romans cruel masters?"

"I think some are and some aren't," I said, "It's a matter of chance."

A slave brought our food and water ration. I tried to get the wounded boy to eat and drink, but he only took a few sips of water, and none of the food. He was burning with fever. He died the next day. "Lucky little bastard," commented the man on my left. I was inclined to agree with him. Few experiences in life are as unpleasant and humiliating as being a prisoner in chains.

After a few days, however, Lucius appeared. He said to one of his soldiers in Latin, "Take this man to my tent. I need to interrogate him."

Lucius's tent looked much like the tent he had occupied at Tarraco. There was, however, a wounded Celtiberian lying on a cot on one side of the tent. He had blue eyes, similar to those of the assassin of Hasdrubal the Fair, whose crucifixion I had witnessed so many years ago. His hair was reddish blond. He nodded and smiled faintly.

Lucius entered the tent and sat down at his table. He did not take out a parchment and stylus but immediately offered me a cup of wine. I took it and sipped it. "Falernian?" I asked.

Lucius grinned. "Very good, Gisco." Then he became serious. "I'm sorry about the chains. I can't openly treat you differently from other prisoners. But, if all goes well, it won't be for too much longer. A delegation of thirty elders has arrived from Carthage to sue for peace. If we can come to an agreement, we will release you and all the other prisoners, all 20,000 of them."

"And if not?" I asked.

"That would be unfortunate, Gisco, both for Carthage and for us. But in any case I won't let you be sold into slavery. I'll buy you myself and set you free."

"That's very kind of you," I said.

Lucius smiled. "I remember you once asked the Scipios what they would do in your situation, and they wouldn't give you an answer. I thought long and hard about what I would have done in your situation and I kept coming to the same conclusion—I would have done the same as you. There was something about what you did that I admired. Are your wife and children in Carthage?"

"Yes," I said.

"Your little Hanno must be big now," he said.

"Yes, he's twelve. I can't believe it's been so long."

"This has been a long war," said Lucius. "Now it's over. I'm looking forward to going back to Rome. But tell me; just what happened to you after I last saw you?"

"Mago had me and my family abducted from Tarraco. He sent Sansara and the children on to Carthage, and restored me to my former duties. I served him until he died, and then I served Hannibal until this battle."

"So they didn't crucify you, after all," said Lucius. "I thought they would. I was amazed to see you at Hannibal's side, but I didn't want to say anything that might get you in trouble with Hannibal."

I smiled. "And I was amazed to see you. I didn't know that you and Publius were that close."

"I've known Publius since I was barely in the *toga virilis*. We trained together on the Field of Mars. I've served under him as military tribune since he went to Spain to take the command in place of his dead father and uncle. You saw those Roman and Italian cavalrymen and how good they were in battle? I trained them."

"I'm impressed," I said, "And here I thought you were just a secretary!"

"I think that you and I are both men to be reckoned with on the battlefield, but now we will each be obliged to develop other skills. Just between you and me, after sixteen years, I'm thoroughly sick of this war, and I'm glad it's over."

I smiled. "I've been sick of this war for a long time. At least you're lucky to be on the winning side. When I was young I saw war as something exciting and glorious, but now I see it for what it is, a nasty business that benefits no one."

"That's what my wife always said. We men don't pay much heed to the women, but perhaps we should." Lucius grinned.

Then the tent flap opened and a man walked in. It took me a moment to recognize Publius Scipio. He looked at the Celtiberian and then at me. "Lucius," he said, "wherever do you come by this penchant for adopting pets? First this Celtiberian, and now a *Poenus*, of all things!"

"Publius," said Lucius, "may I introduce Gisco? He was a deserter from Mago's army, who provided your father and uncle with a gold mine of valuable information. It was a pity that they wasted it all by dying on the battlefield. If you want to ask him questions, he speaks fluent Greek."

Scipio looked at me. "So how was it that you returned to the Carthaginians?"

"Mago found out that I was in Tarraco and had me abducted."

"And he didn't have you crucified?" he asked.

"Evidently not," I smiled, "I had friends in high places."

"Friends in high places wouldn't help a Roman who committed treason no matter who they were," said Scipio.

"But I'm a Carthaginian," I said. "There is no one in Rome with power equivalent to that possessed by Mago Barca."

"Thank all the gods for that!" exclaimed Scipio.

"Publius, sit down and have some wine." Lucius poured Scipio a cup of his Falernian. "There are certain factors that may explain why Mago pardoned Gisco, but we can talk about that later."

"So then, Gisco," said Scipio, sipping his wine, "perhaps you'll answer some questions for me. How long do you think Carthage would be able to hold out in a siege?"

"Carthage is impregnable," I said. "The walls are high and strong all around the city. I happen to know that they've stored enough food to last for years. I was in charge of siege engines at Saguntum, so I know something about sieges. It would take you longer to break down the walls of Carthage than it took Hannibal to destroy the walls of Saguntum, and you would lose a lot of Roman lives in the process."

"Then you would advise us to come to terms with Carthage?" he asked.

"Let's put it this way," I said, "Rome has much to gain by sparing Carthage and making it tributary to you. A siege would be costly of Roman lives and materiel. Yes, you could probably take the city eventually, but it would result in a one-time bounty in booty and slaves. Carthage is a city of merchants; we trade with everyone in the known world. It can be a gold mine for Rome. It can provide Rome with wealth for centuries to come. If you're worried about a military revival, it won't happen. You've taken Spain and the Balearics and you've alienated the Numidian kingdoms from us. We have no other sources of mercenaries."

Scipio looked at me thoughtfully. "Thank you, Gisco. What you say makes sense. I will give it some thought." Then he turned to Lucius. "You may free this man and send him back to Carthage with the delegation of elders."

I was freed from my chains, and Lucius escorted me to where the Carthaginian delegation was camped. One of the delegates was my father. By this time Aba was in his early seventies. He and I embraced, tears running down his cheeks. "All is lost, Gisco," he said. "We are completely at the mercy of the Romans now. Your brother is dead, Caphonbal is dead, and Bomilcar is among the missing. I have very little hope that he survived."

"We just have to hope that the Romans will agree to spare Carthage, Aba," I said. "I think we must agree to everything they demand. Buba was right so many years ago; we should have made peace when we could have done it on favorable terms. Now it's too late."

The Romans laid out their terms of peace, and the elders accepted them. Carthage would not be allowed to wage wars outside of its own territory, and would no longer lay claim to any Islands in the Mediterranean. We were to surrender all elephants, all Roman and allied prisoners, and all deserters. Except for a token number of warships, our entire fleet would be taken out to the harbor and burned. We were to pay a heavy indemnity to Rome of 10,000 talents over the course of the next fifty years.

At the conclusion of the negotiations, I returned to Carthage along with the delegation of elders. The 20,000 prisoners were released. Unfortunately, my nephew, Bomilcar, was not among them, and his body was never found. I was happy that none of my children had been old enough to volunteer. Carthage would be impoverished for a while, but we Carthaginians are talented at acquiring wealth by trade, and we would prosper again in a few years, despite the indemnity we owed to Rome.

SANSARA

"When is my Aba coming home, Uma?" asked Gillimas.

"I don't know, darling," I replied.

I was not at all certain that Gisco would be coming home. Hannibal had arrived the week before with 11,000 survivors of the battle, but Gisco was not among them. Rumor had it that 20,000 had been killed and 20,000 taken prisoner. Even if Gisco were alive and a prisoner he might be sold into slavery and never come home.

Hannibal had urged the Senate to come to an agreement with the Romans, and Gisco's Aba was among the thirty delegates sent to treat with them. They would beg and plead to the Romans to spare Carthage, promising to do whatever the Romans wanted.

Gisco's Uma came to the door of our apartment, still dressed in the somber gray colors of mourning. "Imilce is here to see you, Sansara."

Uma looked to be on the verge of tears. I put my arms around her. "I'm sure Aba will be back soon, Uma. I'll ask Imilce if she has any information." Uma nodded and squeezed my hand.

"Imilce, it's so nice to see you," I said, "how is Hannibal?"

I sent a servant for some bread, fruit, and wine and we sat down on a couch to talk.

"Oh, Sansara, he's depressed and preoccupied," she said. "I think that he feels he's lost his purpose in life. He mourns for Hasdrubal and Mago, and all of the other soldiers that were close to him who died under his command. He blames himself for losing the war, but he also blames Carthage. He has changed, and he is distant toward me. Right now I wish I had stayed in Castulo. I don't think things will ever be the same between us," she paused for a moment. "I shouldn't complain. You don't even know if your Gisco is still alive. I'm sorry, Sansara." The servant arrived with the refreshments and poured us each a cup of wine. I thought, what a fool Hannibal must be, not to see what a wonderful woman he has in Imilce.

"Amashtar's situation is worse than mine," I said. "She lost her husband Drubal and her daughter Caphonbal, and now Bomilcar is among the missing. I think she's on the brink of madness."

"Yes," said Imilce. "It's a pity that she has such disdain for Spanish tribal women and would not allow us to be her friends. She is like Saponibal. If it weren't for you, Sansara, I would have no friends here. At least you and I can comfort each other."

"I'm sorry about Hannibal," I said. "Maybe things will improve with time. Do you hear anything about the negotiations with the Romans?"

"Yes," said Imilce. "Hannibal received a courier last night. The Elders agreed to everything the Romans wanted, and signed a treaty. It's very unfavorable to Carthage, but at least the city will be spared and allowed to rule itself under its own laws. Your father-in-law and the others are on their way home."

"Uma will be happy," I said, "she's been fretting all week. She's not like Saponibal or Amashtar, Imilce. She has always been kind to me, even when I couldn't speak Phoenician. Gisco has such nice parents; it makes me wonder where Drubal came from."

Imilce laughed. "His grandmother, I think. I've heard she was a terror."

Two days later Gisco's Aba came home, and by his side was Gisco! I put my arms around him and wept with relief. He had aged in the three years he had been gone, and he looked weary and undernourished, but he was alive. The children gathered around us and Gisco embraced each of them in turn.

My joy was tarnished only by the misery and obvious hostility of Amashtar. Bomilcar did not return, and Aba told her he had little hope that he was alive. She took out her frustration on me. I tried not to do anything to provoke her, but even asking her to pass a plate of bread provoked an outburst. Gisco's Aba did not like to see disharmony at the dinner table. He said, "Amashtar, why are you not civil to your sister-in-law?"

"She is not my sister-in-law," said Amashtar. "She is just some slut from Spain who has no business being here in Carthage. She has her husband, he is alive. She has her six children. They are alive. I have no one, no one!"

So that was it. "Amashtar, I feel bad for you," I said, "but I never wished you ill, I never wished harm to Drubal or to Caphonbal or to Bomilcar. If you must blame someone for your misfortune, Amashtar, blame the man who caused it. Blame Hannibal. He started this accursed war!"

There. I said it. I finally said it. Everyone in the household stared at me in shock, eyes wide and mouths open. There was complete silence. I stood up and walked out of the room with my head held high.

## GISCO

I couldn't get too angry with Sansara, even though she embarrassed me in front of the family. She's a woman, and as Lucius said, women are different when it comes to matters such as war. I followed her out of the room.

"Sansara, I love you, I really do. But sometimes I wish I hadn't encouraged you to learn Phoenician!" I laughed.

"I only said the truth!" she exclaimed. "The truth!"

"Maybe you're right," I said. "Maybe that is the truth. But people don't want to hear the truth. The truth is we are all going to die. Who wants to hear that? And anyway, it's too late. The truth does us no good now."

"Very well, I won't tell it anymore," she said, "but something needs to be done about Amashtar. How can I live in the same dwelling with her?"

"I will discuss that with Aba," I said. "I'm sure we can find a solution."

In the end Aba placed Amashtar with one of her brothers, and provided her with a dowry so that she might marry again.

Peace has been good to me. I joined Aba in his business ventures, and inherited his estate when he died. My two daughters have married well, and my sons have prospered. I have many grandchildren. Sansara and I have grown old together. Not many couples have that privilege.

Hannibal prospered for a time in Carthage and was even elected *Suffete*, but the old divisions and animosities persisted, and Hannibal, perhaps, tried too hard to accomplish reforms. His enemies plotted to get him into trouble with the Romans, and he was forced to flee Carthage.

He offered his military expertise to Antiochus III, of the Seleucid Empire, who was an enemy of Rome. When the Romans, under Publius Scipio's brother, Lucius, defeated Antiochus, Hannibal fled to Crete.

But Hannibal was never secure thereafter from pursuit by the Romans. Eventually they caught up with him in Bithynia, where King Prusius betrayed him to the Roman Proconsul, Titus Quinctius Flamininus. Hannibal took poison to avoid being captured and brought to Rome in chains.

That is the end of my story.

# GLOSSARY

Disclaimer: Some of the Punic terms are educated guesses on the part of the author. The Phoenician written language has been deciphered to a large degree from inscriptions on stelae, but no one knows the actual pronunciation of words because the Phoenician alphabet lacked vowels. The original Phoenicians lived in what is now Lebanon, just to the north of what is now Israel. Their language and the language of the ancient Hebrews was were probably close enough to have been mutually intelligible. Modern Arabic is a related Semitic language but more distant from Phoenician and Hebrew. Punic terms that I'm uncertain of will be marked with an asterisk.

Aba*: Punic term for father.

Alif Bet*: The Punic alphabet.

Baal Hammon: A Carthaginian god.

Barca: The surname of Hamilcar Barca, passed on to his sons, Hannibal, Hasdrubal and Mago. Literally means "thunderbolt."

Buba*: Punic term for grandmother.

Bucina: Roman trumpets, used for giving signals to soldiers on the battlefield.

Byrsa: The citadel of Carthage. Similar to the Acropolis in Athens.

Cornua: Roman battle horns.

Cothon: One of two harbors of Carthage.

Decurion: A Roman military officer. One of three such officers who commanded a *turma* or unit of thirty cavalrymen.

Domus: A Latin term for house.

Edepol: A mild oath. Derives from Pollux, one of the pair of twin gods, Castor and Pollux.

Elissa: The founder and Queen of Carthage. Also called Dido.

Ephebos: A Greek term for a young man.

Eques: A Roman of the wealthiest plebeian class. Filled the ranks of the Roman cavalry.

Eshmoun: Carthaginian god of healing, roughly equivalent to the Greek god Aesclepius.

Falarica: Javelin used by the defenders of Saguntum. The shaft was coated with pitch and set afire before being hurled.

Falcata: An ancient Spanish sword, similar to the Greek Kopis. (The term is a linguistic anachronism which dates only to the 19th century. The original term is unknown.)

Falernian: Refers to a wine made from grapes from the Falernian region of Italy south of Rome. Considered the best wine of its era.

Hastati: The first line in a traditional Roman military formation, consisting of light armed and relatively inexperienced troops.

Hubris: A Greek term for a fatal personal flaw brought about by arrogance.

Ishtar: A Carthaginian goddess of fertility, borrowed from neighboring peoples of Cyprus and Crete.

Khart Hadasht: Punic name for Carthage and New Carthage. Literally means "New City." Used only for New Carthage (Spain) in this book.

Kyrios: Respectful Greek term of address for men.

Megara: A suburb of Carthage where wealthy people had their mansions.

Melqart: Literally, "God of the City." Punic god similar to Hercules in appearance.

Numidian: Literally nomad. The term refers to various peoples of northern Africa who were Berber in origin and who were recruited as mercenary soldiers during the First and Second Punic wars. After the Second Punic war their leader, Masinissa, established a strong kingdom which attacked Carthage in 150 B.C. giving the Romans a pretext for the Third Punic War.

Poenus: Plural Poeni. The Roman term for a Phoenician or Carthaginian.

Principes: The second line of the traditional Roman Military formation. More experienced and more heavily armed than the *hastati*.

Proconsul: A Roman provincial governor with consular authority.

Pugio: A dagger used by Roman soldiers.

Quinquereme: A Greek, Roman, or Carthaginian ship propelled by five banks or oars on either side.

Rab: Punic term of respect. Also means leader or chief.

Rab Kohanim: Punic term for chief priest.

Rab Mahanet: Punic term for supreme military leader.

Shekel*: Carthaginian monetary unit.

Tablinum: A room in a Roman house where business is conducted.

Tanit: A female Punic goddess, consort to Baal Hammon.

Suffete: One of two annually elected chief magistrates in ancient Carthage.

Triarii: The third line of the standard Roman military formation. These were the oldest and most experienced soldiers.

Uma*: Punic term for mother.

Viniae: Covered walkways which were part of a siege operation, protecting the soldiers attempting to besiege a city.

# BIBLIOGRAPHY


Ancient sources.

Titus Livius. Ab Urbe Condita. c 25 A.D. Translated by D. Spillan and Cyrus Edmonds.

Polybius. The Rise of Rome. c 150 B.C. Translated by Ian Scott- Kilvert.

Appian of Alexandria. Roman History. c 150 A.D. Translated by John Carter.

Lucius Mestrius Plutarchus. Lives of Noble Greeks and Romans. c 100 A.D. Translated by Arthur Hugh Clough and John Dryden.

Modern Sources

Abott, Jacob. Hannibal, The Greatest Commander. Harper Brothers, 1876.

Cottrell, Leonard. Hannibal, Enemy of Rome. First Da Capo Press, 1992.

Daly, Gregory. Cannae, The Experience of Battle in the Second Punic War. Routledge, 2002.

Dodge, Theodore Ayrault. Hannibal. Tale End Press, 2012

Garland, Robert. Hannibal. Bristol Classical Press, 2010.

Gabriel, Richard. Scipio Africanus, Rome's Greatest General. Potomac Books Incorporated, 2007.

Goldsworthy, Adrian. The Fall of Carthage. Phoenix, 2006.

Goldsworthy, Adrian. The Punic Wars. Cassell, 2000.

Hoyos, Dexter. The Carthaginians. Routledge Press, 2010.

Lazenby, J.F. Hannibal's War. University of Oklahoma Press, 1998.

Liddle Hart, B.F. Scipio Africanus: Greater Than Napoleon. W.Blackwood and Sons, London, 1926.

Miles, Richard. Carthage Must Be Destroyed. Viking Penguin, 2010.

Robert L. The Ghosts of Cannae. Random House, 2010.

Scullard, H.H. Scipio Africanus: Soldier and Politician. Cornell University Press, 1970.